SHADOW SWORN

SHADOW SWORN

DRAGON OF SHADOW AND AIR BOOK TWO

JESS MOUNTIFIELD

DISRUPTIVE IMAGINATION

For all the amazing folks on my Discord. You've sprinted with me, played games with me and been there at all the strange times of the day and night when I needed people to talk to

LMBPN Publishing
PMB 196, 2540 South Maryland Pkwy
Las Vegas, NV 89109

Version 1.10 April 2021
eBook ISBN: 978-1-64971-720-7
Print ISBN: 978-1-64971-721-4

THE SHADOW SWORN TEAM

Thanks to our JIT Team:

Dorothy Lloyd
Dave Hicks
Rachel Beckford
John Ashmore
Zacc Pelter
Deb Mader
Veronica Stephan-Miller
Diane L. Smith
Kelly O'Donnell
Larry Omans
Misty Roa
Paul Westman

If we've missed anyone, please let us know!

Editor
SkyHunter Editing Team

CHAPTER ONE

Releasing the pent-up energy I held, I jumped off the platform. A blast of air shot out from my hands toward the ground. For a moment it lifted me up, stopping me from falling.

The part-elven nature within me allowed me to reach out and control air. Right now, I was trying to use it to fly —with limited success.

I overbalanced and rolled forward. As I tried to compensate by moving my hands, I wobbled more and more.

After a few seconds of teetering in the air, I fell to the mat below. Exhaling, I lay there for a moment, not ready to try again.

"That was your longest attempt yet, Aella," Minsheng said as he came over to me. He offered me a hand to help me up.

When I got to my feet, I noticed Zephyr, the dragon I'd bonded with, had laid down to watch. I sighed. Was I ever going to be able to use my abilities to fly?

"Why don't we have lunch and come back to it again this afternoon?" Minsheng suggested.

He received no argument from me. I'd been training all morning, and despite getting stronger, it was still draining to use my powers for so much of the day. It was no doubt made worse by trying to do something new. Flying required a lot more power and concentration than anything else I had tried to do.

No sooner had we sat down at the small table in the far corner than Minsheng's sister Daisy appeared with a tray full of food, a late breakfast. It was simple fare, but there was plenty of it.

Zephyr got to his feet and hurried over. There was only one thing he liked more than eating, and that was flying.

It was just a shame that Zephyr was getting too big to easily fly around in the training room we had. Although we'd rebuilt the room and rearranged a few things, it just wasn't big enough anymore.

Zephyr was now roughly the size of a motorbike, and almost as tall as me when he held his head erect. If you counted his tail, he was now longer, and he had an appetite to match. By far, the biggest bowl of food was for Zephyr.

"I barely feel like I'm getting anywhere," I said as I tucked into the chow mein.

"It's only been four days," Minsheng replied. "And you're trying to do something incredibly difficult. Not only do you need to draw on more power than normal, but you need to combine that with balance and your body's ability to hold you in a stiff pose and direct the airflow. That's four different things at once."

Minsheng's words made me feel a little bit better about

my failure so far. But only a little. Ever since I'd read the story and seen the pictures where Tuviel and Azargad had flown together, I'd wanted to learn to fly with my own abilities. Just because it was hard didn't mean I was satisfied with my lack of progress.

I had been obsessed with the famous bonded elf and dragon ever since learning they were my ancestors. It was the first time I'd had any idea who I was related to, even if they'd lived thousands of years earlier.

"Did the organization send that book on dragon development and genetic memory?" I asked.

"Apparently it's in the post. But who knows how long it will actually take to get here? I think it's coming from Korea."

I lifted my eyebrows, but I didn't bother asking for an explanation. From what I'd gathered from Minsheng's mentions of the organization, It wasn't a headquarters somewhere but a group of people scattered around the globe who tried to protect the mythical and fairytale-like creatures and races wherever they appeared. That included me.

Only eight weeks ago, I'd thought I was a normal person, but now I knew I was anything but. The organization had tested samples of my DNA. I was part dragon, part elf, and part human. If I'd known who my real parents were, I'd have asked them why I'd only learned this in my late twenties. Instead, I had to satisfy myself with learning everything I could from Minsheng.

The first hint that the world had not been normal had been when I'd found Zephyr as an egg in an abandoned warehouse. I'd bonded with him not long before he hatched, and we'd been together ever since. At first, we'd been on the run from a shadow agency, one that wanted to hide people and creatures like us from the rest of the world. Minsheng and his friend had helped me send them a message.

They now left us alone as long as we remained hidden. So here we were, in a training room underneath a restaurant in Chinatown in LA.

"Is there someone you can ask about controlling the air with more precision?" I asked Minsheng, still thinking about how I could fly.

"No. Sorry," Minsheng replied. "No one within the organization has trained anyone with air elemental magic in at least two decades."

I dropped my spoon. What did he mean, no one had trained anyone for the last two decades?

"You have to understand everyone has been in hiding. There are rumors of a sanctuary. A place where many people like you and me have banded together and now live in a safe little community, but they're rumors. Agencies like the one here in LA are all over the world."

I frowned. How exactly was Minsheng going to train me if he had no experience with my abilities? The day we'd first met, he'd told me he'd been waiting for me his whole life. I'd thought that meant he knew everything I needed to know. But over the last few weeks, I'd realized that in some matters, he was as deep in the dark as I was. The governments of the world had made sure of it.

In a lot of ways, I couldn't blame him. He was doing his best, but it didn't keep me from being frustrated. I wanted to learn faster. To be the best I could be. I had a nagging doubt that at some point, Zephyr would get so large, or we would slip up in some way, and the agency would be right back to hunting us.

As soon as I'd finished eating, I got to my feet again.

"Before you go right back to learning to fly, I did get one new thing from the organization today," Minsheng said.

He went over to a small cupboard at the end of the room and pulled out a package. It was already open, and he showed me the contents.

"This belongs to you," Minsheng said as he held up a necklace. "At least, the organization believes it does."

I took it from him, surprised at first that the metal the chain was made of was warm. It seemed to tingle against my skin. I reached for the pendant, turning it so I could see the front. Wrought in the same metal was a dragon eye with a white gem set into its center. As I rested it against my palm, the gem seemed to glow.

"It's enchanted. Although as an elf, you heal quicker than most, while wearing this, a lot of your natural elven abilities and your link with Zephyr should be enhanced. Think of it as a signal booster to everything elven."

"But how do they know it is mine?" I asked.

"It belonged to Tuviel. As her strongest living relative the organization knows about, they thought you'd better have it."

My mouth fell open. I'd just inherited something extremely valuable. I looked for a clasp to put the necklace on, but there was none. I turned to Minsheng to ask how to get it on, the loop too small to fit over a head, but he was absorbed in reading a note.

"It seems that if you have enough of Tuviel's blood in you, you can pinch the slightly longer link at the top, and it will open." Minsheng pointed to the link he meant.

"No pressure, then," I replied.

At first, I wasn't sure I wanted to even try. For a moment, I'd been hopeful that this was the organization accepting me as Tuviel's heir. Instead, it seemed like a sort of test. I would be returning the necklace if they weren't right in trusting me.

Zephyr came closer and leaned his head against my midsection, his way of giving me a cuddle. Sometimes it seemed like Zephyr had a sixth sense about my emotions.

Taking a deep breath, I reached for the link. All my fears vanished in a fraction of a second as it fell open. It seemed I was descended from Tuviel after all. Unable to keep the grin from creeping across my face, I put the necklace around my neck. As if it sensed what I was intending and where it was, the necklace snapped shut, now fixed firmly in place.

I felt warmth spread through my body, starting from the dragon pendant as it rested against my chest and radiating outward to my extremities. Whatever the necklace did, it felt like I'd just got stronger.

I looked at Minsheng to find him studying me. Before I could ask anything more about it, Minsheng looked away, busying himself with packing away the empty box and the small note that had come with the necklace.

"I'd best get back to training," I said, wondering if the necklace would help me with what I'd been attempting to learn. I could only hope.

Try it standing, a voice said in my head. I looked around.

Had I heard that? Had that been out loud? I heard a dry sort of chuckle.

Zephyr, was that you? I thought as I looked at him. He had a strange look on his scaly face as if he was studying me, but his mouth hung slightly open like he was grinning.

Yes. That was me. The second you put that necklace on, it was like the bond between us grew.

But you can't talk. You've never said a word.

No, I can't talk. You're just hearing voices in your head and going crazy. As I heard those words, Zephyr rolled his eyes.

"Minsheng," I said to get my mentor's attention. "Is there supposed to be a telepathic link between an elf and their bonded creature?"

Minsheng looked at the two of us.

You're not going crazy. Zephyr rolled his eyes again. *I was led to believe that the human world understood sarcasm.*

I do. I just wasn't expecting to hear you in my head. No one mentioned that this was possible.

They might not have known.

"You two are talking to each other, aren't you?" Minsheng asked.

I nodded. "It would seem so."

"Interesting." Minsheng rushed to the bookshelves in the far corner and pulled out a particularly large leather-bound tome. It was almost falling apart.

As I walked slowly over to join him, he leafed through the pages. By the time I was beside him, he had found the page he was looking for and stopped to read it.

The book wasn't in a language I recognized, so I had to wait patiently for him to tell me what it said. I wasn't good at that.

7

"What does it say?" I asked when a few minutes later, he still hadn't said anything.

"This book was written about a decade after Tuviel and Azargad were dead. The writer was someone who knew them both and realized that with their deaths, the world had lost a great deal of information. They put down everything they knew about Tuviel's magic and the special bond the two of them shared."

"Why didn't I know about this book?" I asked.

"Because their friend was a dwarf, and the book is written in Dwarvish."

"Oh." I sat down on the nearest chair, waiting for Minsheng to explain what was on the pages.

"There's not a lot in here about that aspect of the bond, but the writer does suggest that Azargad and Tuviel shared some kind of telepathic link. The writer suggests that it was either that or they had trained together for so long and developed a set of unique ways of communicating in battle, and in the air especially, that one could let the other know exactly what to do."

"I guess they were telepathic too then."

They were, Zephyr said in my head. *I can remember it. I can remember the sound of her voice when she spoke in my head. Well, not* my *head.*

Let me guess, genetic memory.

I believe that's your term for it.

"Zephyr tells me they did."

"He's actually talking to you?" Minsheng asked as if he'd just realized there was something more fascinating in the room than the book in his hands.

I nodded, grinning smugly. At least that part of my day

was going okay. I was definitely descended from Tuviel, and Zephyr was definitely descended from Azargad. Now I just had to become as powerful as her.

Now perhaps my training would go better. Either way, I was ready to try again.

I climbed up to the small platform a couple of yards off the ground and began sucking in energy, ready to push the air in the opposite direction I wanted to go. At least, that was roughly how I thought this should work.

Push yourself up and off the platform rather than jumping, Zephyr suggested. *It should be easier.*

I tried to focus on what Zephyr suggested, standing on the platform instead of jumping. Slowly I pushed out from my hands, trying to use them like jets. At first the streams weren't strong enough to lift me, but I slowly increased the pressure until my arms were fighting against the up-blast.

To help hold me steady, I tried to lock my arms straight. As I did, I applied a little bit more pressure again. My body lifted off the platform, but that's when everything started to go wrong.

As I tilted one way and tried to compensate, it sent me the other way. Again I tried to rebalance myself. This time I flew off to the side, leaving the platform entirely.

As I shut my powers off, too frustrated to continue, I fell onto the mat.

"That looked more controlled," Minsheng said.

"I don't care," I replied. "I've had enough."

Getting to my feet, I checked the time. It was late evening, although not as late as it often was when I took Zephyr to the beach for some extra exercise. He was so large now he couldn't fly enough inside the building. While we waited for the organization to find and pay for a much larger space, our only option was to head to the beach when it was the most quiet, in the dead of night.

Come on, Zephyr, I thought. *Let's go out.*

Early?

Early. If I try again and fail, I'm going to break something... and probably not me.

I relayed the plan to Minsheng, pretending I hadn't seen the frown of disapproval on his face as he glanced at the clock. Nothing he said would stop me, so there was no point letting him speak and waste his breath.

We hadn't had trouble in weeks, and I'd already checked the weather forecast. There were supposed to be thick clouds all night. Tonight would be far safer than many previous nights had been.

CHAPTER TWO

Behind the wheel of the car, I relaxed since I'd left everything and everyone but Zephyr behind at the restaurant.
This was the only part of the day I got to think, entirely
alone. Well, except for Zephyr. Mostly. But I would pull up
in the parking lot, open the back door, and Zephyr would
fly away for a while.

I kept an eye on him, of course, but it gave us both some
much-needed space. It wasn't ideal, but given our
constraints, it was good enough. The rest of the time I was
either training or working in the restaurant.

Ever since Minsheng had taken me in officially, I'd
offered to work doing several waitressing shifts a week. It
gave me a way to earn some money and pay my adopted
parents and everyone I'd borrowed stuff from or stolen
from when I'd been on the run back. It had even allowed
me to buy myself a few luxuries.

Of course, I didn't have to pay for very much since my
room and food came with the training, but they didn't pay
me very much either. Given it was the first time I had a

waitressing job where I liked my boss, I considered it a win.

I smiled as I thought about the better elements of my life right now and got out of the car. I might be frustrated with my training progress, but I'd never been happier.

While I stood, already calming, Zephyr flew into the clouds, momentarily lost from my sight. I wondered how much more content I could be if we didn't have to hide in the shadows.

What would our lives look like if people knew we existed? Would we be able to walk around in daylight? Or were dragons just too scary?

I asked myself these kinds of questions almost every evening, but I didn't have the answers. Part of me wanted to trust in the goodness of humanity. I wanted to believe that if humans knew about us, they would be accepting, but I feared they wouldn't. I feared the agency that had hunted us had been right.

As Zephyr dived out of the cloud, I looked up. He unfurled his wings only a couple of yards above me, a single powerful downbeat enough to keep him from crashing into the sand.

I didn't know you could do that move, I thought, hoping he'd hear me.

This ability to communicate with you wasn't the only memory that came to me recently. I have memories of flying, of learning to fly the last time. I think many memories are still locked away, but flying now seems very natural, like I've been doing it for thousands of years.

How long do dragons live? I asked.

I don't know. It's hard to tell. The memories are not always of the same ancestor, but I think we live longer than humans. We have mourned many people.

I'm sorry. That must be hard.

Sometimes yes, Zephyr replied. As he did that, I realized he was speaking in an adult's voice. The voice of someone who had lived many decades, not the voice of a child. This dragon had only been alive for a few weeks, yet here he was, talking about grief like a seasoned adult who had lost many friends to the ravages of time.

I also remember many good things, but no memory is as strong or carries the same emotion as the moment I saw your face for the first time. The smile you gave me and the light in your eyes.

It's also one of my best memories.

A rush of warmth spread through me as I thought back to the moment I'd sat inside the abandoned shopping mall, hiding in a derelict shop, holding his egg as he hatched. My world had changed forever that day.

Run with me? He landed, lightly spraying me with sand. *Let's head down the beach together.*

I opened my mouth to object since my body was still a little sore from the failed flying attempts, but instead of saying no, I shut my mouth and nodded. I started running the way he was facing. The sandy beach gave way beneath each footfall, making me work harder to move forward.

As if sensing this difficulty, Zephyr took a diagonal path closer to the waves, where the sand was wetter and more firm. Soon we were racing each other, his body more powerful but equally badly designed for running across the sand.

At first I pulled ahead, my heart rate increasing as I

pounded across the sand, but I was far better at sprinting fast over short distances. The farther we went, the more I slowed, until Zephyr overtook me, his body far fitter and stronger than mine.

For a moment I watched him pull away, and then I reached for the familiar part of me that could take control of the air. Using it to buffet me along from behind, I eased the strain on my muscles and once again sped up.

I grinned as I overtook him.

Cheater, his voice boomed in my head.

You're a dragon. Only way I'll even come close as you continue to get bigger, I replied.

He laughed and launched into the air, his shadow over me momentarily before he flew ahead. I slowed, out of breath and beginning to feel tired from the constant use of magic. I'd never trained as hard in my life as I had for the last few weeks. Every night I fell into bed so exhausted I was pretty much asleep before my head hit the pillow.

Each week I noticed I was stronger, however, and not just in my control of the air. Physically, I'd never been in better shape. I was also eating better and more regularly. My body had become more muscular and toned, and it took longer for me to get out of breath.

Once more watching Zephyr fly and desperate to be up there with him, I sighed. If I didn't master flying, it wouldn't be many more weeks before he would be large and strong enough to bear my weight, but there was something reassuring about the idea of being able to fly myself.

More than once, I'd had the nightmare thought that in a fight, I could be knocked off his back. If it happened on a day like today, I'd plummet to my death.

I shuddered at the mental image, but before I could even begin to attempt to distract myself, Zephyr suddenly darted to the right, out to sea. It was like someone had tugged on a string inside me and pulled something important out of my body.

What's happening? I asked, hoping the new mental link between us stretched that far.

Company. They saw me. Saw us.

Shitsticks.

Yup. I'll stay out to sea for a bit. There's a group of them walking your way.

Noted.

I kept walking, but I slowed to give my breathing time to recover. Despite my skills and abilities, I was a lone woman on a beach in the middle of the night. Zephyr had failed to mention the makeup of the group. Were they all men?

I didn't have to wonder for long before they came into view. It was a mixed group, three girls and two guys, all wearing shorts and hooded sweatshirts.

They were laughing and joking, meandering along the beach my way.

"I swear it was this way," one of them said. "And it was definitely..."

When I was spotted, the young man's voice trailed off.

"Hi," I said. "Nice evening for a walk."

I wouldn't normally have been so bold, but I suspected they were talking about Zephyr.

"Have you seen anything...funky?" one of them asked.

"Not unless you count a couple of seagulls making

babies." I kept walking as I talked. "Why? Are you out hunting UFOs?"

The group exchanged glances, none of them seeming to know how to respond. I stopped as if I was curious.

"You *have* seen something?" I asked.

"Dale here thinks he saw a dragon. We all think he's been drinking too much."

"Sounds like you might have been. More likely to see the Loch Ness monster than a dragon." I grinned as if this was the funniest thing ever, waved, and kept walking.

If they only thought they'd seen a dragon, then I didn't have an awful lot to worry about. It wasn't hard proof, and it wasn't anything that was going to get me in trouble with the agency.

As I moved farther away and the sound of them receded into the background, so did my fears. The waves grew louder as I got to a section of beach that was stonier.

Is it safe to come back yet? Zephyr asked in my head.

I looked behind before answering. I could just about make out the group. They'd formed a huddle as if they were gathered around something several hundred yards away. While I was looking at them, I could have sworn one of them glanced at me.

Not yet. Let me get farther away.

I kept walking, somehow not at ease. Had they seen Zephyr? They didn't seem to be telling me everything. But who would tell a complete stranger?

Trying to tell myself I was probably just being paranoid, I walked a little farther and glanced back again. The teenagers were gone, or at least far enough up the beach that they were lost in the shadows.

Safe now, I said. It was still strange to be talking to Zephyr without saying anything, but it definitely saved a lot of effort.

He didn't reply, but soon I felt more normal again, the strange feeling in my torso fading until I saw the shadow of his wings as he flew down and landed beside me again.

I reached out and stroked him, beginning to feel very tired but relieved.

"We need to find a safe way back to the car," I said aloud. He nodded, and the two of us set off. We moved higher up the beach. It was nearer the buildings, but it gave us more places to hide and reduced the sound of the waves so we'd be more likely to hear someone coming.

We didn't get very far before I spotted the teenagers lingering up the beach.

I froze, not sure how to get us back without Zephyr being seen.

Why don't I hide somewhere in the opposite direction? His voice boomed in my head, almost making me jump. *You can get the car and come meet me.*

It was a far better suggestion than any of the possibilities running through my head. After giving him the affirmative and watching him turn back around and slip away, I slowly walked off.

Going in the opposite direction from Zephyr felt strange again. I'd rarely left him anywhere or had him out of my sight since he'd hatched. Even when we came out here, I was usually looking in the direction he'd traveled or knew which cloud he was flying behind.

This time as Zephyr went one way and I went the other, I felt like an invisible string was unraveling from a coil in the middle of my stomach, taking a small piece of me with it as the distance between us grew. It wasn't comfortable and mirrored the feeling I'd had earlier, only this time it was slower and less surprising.

I was so distracted by the growing separation that I didn't notice the teenagers at first. They hadn't moved for some time, staring at something on a phone still.

I was only a few dozen feet away when they looked at me again. I waved and smiled.

"Are you lost?" I asked, knowing the answer would probably be no but wanting to make it clear their actions looked suspicious. "I've lived here awhile. Do you need directions?"

Again they exchanged glances, but none of them seemed to want to answer my question. They weren't playing this one cool at all.

I shrugged as if I was a little perplexed by them but not worried about their behavior. Still walking, I tried to put them out of my mind and focus on my link with Zephyr. The distance between us would be a good test of how well and how far we could communicate telepathically.

Can you still hear me? I asked a moment later.

Yes, but I have to concentrate. His words echoed my sentiments, the voice in my head no longer sounding quite as natural.

I couldn't help but look over my shoulder several more times. Every time I did, the teenagers were still there. It seemed like they were following me, keeping their distance and trying to act natural but not succeeding.

I knew I was probably just paranoid, but I sped up a fraction, eager to get back to the car. The next time I glanced behind, I tried to be more subtle and not draw attention to it. Still the teenagers came with me.

If you can still hear me, Zephyr, I think those kids might be a problem. They're following me.

Your words are faint. I'm trying to find somewhere to hide. This area of the beach is more lit up, and there are more people.

Zephyr's words made me frown. This night felt like it was going from bad to worse.

As I neared the car, I knew I needed to check how close the teenagers were again. Thoughts of muggings or worse ran through my head when I saw they were even closer to me. What game were they playing? Did they realize how intimidated I felt?

I pulled my keys from my pocket, unlocked the car, and quickly got inside. Sand came off my shoes, falling all over the interior.

"Sorry, Minsheng," I said under my breath as I stuck the key in the ignition.

The teenagers hurried over to a car of their own as I quickly pulled out of my space and tried my best to get out of the parking lot before they could follow.

Thankfully, they took so long to get in the car that I was long gone and out of sight. Only then did I relax.

I'm coming. Just hold on a little longer, Zephyr. I'm on my way.

CHAPTER THREE

It felt like I drove forever before the bond with Zephyr returned enough for us to easily talk to each other.

Are you safe? I asked as soon as I could feel his presence in my head once more.

For now.

That was all the information he gave me. Part of me wanted to beg for more, to ask if he was going to be safe until I could get to him. I also wanted to know if he thought anyone else had seen him. But I was more concerned about getting him into the car and back to the restaurant

I made a mental note not to come back out at this time of night. In the future, we would wait like we always did.

As I drove, I could feel the bond between Zephyr and me grow stronger. It calmed me and made me feel like everything was once more right in my world.

There are a lot of people here. They seem to be searching for something. I don't think it's me, but I'm not sure what they are looking for. Is this a normal human thing? Zephyr asked.

I don't think so. Not at this time of night.

I tried to imagine what a bunch of humans could be doing on a beach at one in the morning. I couldn't, especially not if they were looking for something.

What makes you think they're looking? Did they have metal detectors?

No, just flashlights. They keep going over the same bits of beach, and occasionally one of them cries out like they found something. I think whatever it is keeps escaping.

I blinked as I drove. As I rounded the final corner, I thought I could see what Zephyr meant. A group of humans had fanned out along the beach in pairs. They were clearly searching, some of them stopping to dig, but most of them directing the beams of their flashlights back and forth as they scanned the sand.

Pulling into the parking lot there, I shut the engine off and got out. I couldn't see Zephyr, but given the activity, I didn't blame him for not wanting to come out.

Was he what the teenagers had seen? Or was this something else?

I'm safe for now, but I pity whatever they're chasing. It clearly doesn't want to be caught.

How big do you think it is?

About the size of a large rat. Whatever it is, they're trying to catch it in some kind of box or cage.

Not sure what else to do, I watched for a while. They were all too busy with their task to notice they had an audience.

I'd only been there for a few minutes when a familiar-looking car pulled into the parking lot. I ducked, not wanting the agents in the black sedan to notice me.

Agents, I informed Zephyr.

Great. Just what we needed, more people to avoid.

I nodded before I remembered that Zephyr couldn't see my reaction, especially since I was hiding between two parked cars.

While I watched, the agents got out of their cars, wearing sunglasses despite the darkness, and made their way onto the sand.

"We hear you've found some kind of endangered sala-mander," the chubbier agent on the left said. As he did, the man on the right had a quick look around. I ducked even lower so the car hood would shield me from view.

"No salamander I've ever seen. It can change color almost instantly, and I'm pretty sure it spits acid," a man replied. "It burned through Griff's jacket. See?"

I looked up in time to see the man hold up a checked flannel jacket. It had a large hole with frayed-looking edges and several smaller holes. Whatever the creature had done, I was starting to suspect it wasn't a salamander. If the agency was here, it must be another creature like Zephyr and me.

Can you see the creature they're looking for? I asked my companion, still not sure where he was or if he could get a better view of what was happening on the beach than I could.

No, but it's sneaky and not very large. It evades them more than they spot it.

We should help it.

Of course. I believe it's also injured.

We're definitely helping it.

Zephyr chuckled, and I looked closely when the agents

went back to their vehicle for a moment. I wasn't sure if they were calling for help or asking for backup; one of them was on his radio for some time.

I had just decided I needed to do something when a shout rose from the beach, not far from where I was. The agents hurried over as three men and a woman tried to corner a creature I could barely see.

It did look a little like a salamander or a newt, but this one was a deep green color one moment and blended with the sand the next. It was clear this wasn't a normal creature, and I knew I had to help it. If the agency caught it, who knew what would happen to it?

Creeping away from the cars, I tried to keep an eye on where it was. How was I going to catch it? If the humans couldn't do so easily, what made me think I could?

The only thing I had in common with this creature was that I didn't belong in this world either. Not entirely. But how did I let it know I was safe?

Use your magic.

Zephyr's suggestion made me wonder if he'd heard my previous thoughts.

Be careful and gentle. We don't want to draw the attention of the agents, just the salamander.

Taking my time, I kept an eye on the humans and the agents racing around the beach. Slowly, I sucked in a gentle breeze and sent it out across the sand.

I tried to keep the force light but consistent, just strange enough that someone who knew people could control the air would pick up on the possibility and look for me. I just had to hope the agents weren't paying that much attention.

For some time, it seemed to have no effect. Just as I was

thinking of giving up and trying something else, the salamander stopped. It looked straight at me and I gave it a small nod before backing up and gesturing to the car.

The stationary creature was almost caught, a human with a box coming within two feet of it. I bit my lip as I could only watch the poor thing run away. It needed to get to me somehow.

Now would be a good time to get into the car, I told Zephyr.

That poor guy needs a distraction first.

We can't make it obvious we're here.

I wasn't planning on making it obvious. But if we don't do something, he's going to run toward us anyway, and we're all going to get caught.

It was a good point, even if I hated to admit it. The agents would follow the salamander straight to us. I wasn't sure I could get out of the parking lot before they'd notice, and I'd promised the woman in charge of the agency I wouldn't interfere.

Without thinking, I'd already interfered. Now we needed to get away with it.

Out of the corner of my eye, I saw Zephyr creep out from behind a car on the far edge of the parking lot toward one of the shops.

What are you thinking? I asked, but he didn't answer. Instead, he stuck a claw under the shutter in front of one of the shops and yanked it up as hard as he could.

He then lifted into the air, catching the glass with his tail. The alarm went off, drawing the attention of everyone on the beach. Of course, they all looked at the shop, but Zephyr was already flying several yards above it.

It wasn't perfect. If anyone looked up, they'd see the shadowy figure of Zephyr as he climbed toward the clouds.

Thankfully he made it there in time, everyone distracted by the alarms. I got into the car, noticing that the agents were less distracted and still looking for the salamander. No doubt they hoped to catch it while everyone else was wondering what happened.

The salamander was clever, however. It burrowed into the sand not far from a box one of the people had put down, and while the agents were looking in a different direction, it came out the other side. I kept the car door partially open and reached down to the ground.

Trying to act as a guide, I slowly blew a jet of air toward the salamander. It picked up on it immediately and hurtled toward me. As it came closer, I could see that it was limping, only three legs pulling it along.

It didn't hesitate to climb inside the car, and I shut the door as soon as it had.

I've got it, I told Zephyr. *Are you safe?*

I'm farther up the beach again. When things have died down a bit, you'll need to come get me.

I'd been about to leave, but Zephyr's words made me cautious. Of course it would look suspicious if I left right now. Instead, I kept an eye on the agents who were still combing the beach and turned toward the salamander.

It had climbed up onto the passenger seat, and it now looked at me.

"Hi there," I said. "You're safe here."

I don't know if it understood me, but it settled down, panting. I waited for a few more minutes, then some of the humans gave up on searching for the salamander, and even the agents looking like they'd had enough.

More than a little anxious to get back to Zephyr, and with the strange tugging sensation in my stomach, I turned the engine on and pulled away.

The salamander perked up, trying to see where we were going.

"We're just going to go get my friend," I said in case he understood me. "He provided that little distraction for us."

I wasn't sure the salamander understood, but for now, he was content to watch the lights go by as I drove up the beach again. By the time I pulled into the parking lot at the top, I was yawning.

No sooner had I opened the car door than Zephyr landed. He quickly got inside, squeezing through the gap. It wasn't long before he had settled down in the back.

The salamander turned to him and gave a strange little half-roar. Zephyr responded, and as I drove away, the two had a sort of conversation.

"Translation?" I asked.

He's only a child, Zephyr sent to my mind. *He's been separated from his family, and the first person to catch him injured his leg. It might be broken. It's why he didn't get away when his family did.*

Let him know we'll help him get better and find them.

Already did. Also, he's hungry.

What do salamanders eat?

Food.

I rolled my eyes but didn't reply, concentrating on getting us back.

As I pulled into the small parking lot behind the restaurant, I noticed the lights were on. Before the engine was even off, Minsheng rushed out.

"You were gone a very long time," Minsheng said, the closest he'd come saying he was worried.

"Some teenagers got in the way, and then we ended up rescuing this little fella." I opened the passenger door to reveal the salamander.

Minsheng raised his eyebrows but didn't comment.

Zephyr got out of the car, and the salamander followed. As soon as Minsheng saw that it was limping, his eyes went wider, and he knelt on the ground to pick the small thing up.

At first the salamander seemed wary, but Zephyr said something to it, letting out several small noises. It hopped onto Minsheng's hand.

As one, we headed inside. Daisy was still up, wringing her hands in the kitchen. A bowl of snacks sat on the countertop beside her.

She sighed with relief when she saw us, until she noticed the injured salamander in Minsheng's hands. This galvanized her into action.

As Minsheng put the small creature on the table, she rushed to a cabinet and pulled out a small first-aid kit. On closer inspection, I saw this wasn't the normal first-aid kit. There were splints and contraptions clearly intended for birds and ointments with strange names. This kit was clearly supposed to be used for animals or creatures of the mythical variety.

While I wondered how many other creatures the family must have helped for this to be a normal item in the house, she set about checking the creature and the injured limb.

"I think it's broken," Daisy said. "But not badly. I haven't got a small enough splint, but I could probably make something."

Zephyr passed the information along, and the salamander seemed to nod. He laid his head down and exhaled. Although I couldn't be sure, I thought he looked tired.

While Daisy busied herself finding a popsicle stick and cutting it short enough, Minsheng readied a small bandage to hold it in place. I found a saucer and filled it with water before carrying it over to the salamander and placing it in front of him.

He eagerly drank, his pink tongue lapping up the water. As he did, he changed color to a paler blue.

Remember, he's hungry as well, Zephyr sent to my mind.

I nodded. *hat do salamanders eat?*

Salad and meat. Much like me.

Pretty much anything, then. I wandered to the fridge and had a look at what was inside. So many of my meals were prepared by other people that I wasn't sure what I'd find. But as I lifted a cucumber and an apple to see what was behind them, the salamander made a noise.

I held up the apple, and the creature nodded.

After finding a chopping board, I cut it into small pieces, stuck them on a plate, and carried it over to him.

While they splinted his leg, he chowed down on the apple chunks. I felt a small amount of pride that we'd managed to rescue the little thing.

By the time everyone was done, I was yawning every few minutes. I wasn't the only one.

"We should all get some rest. You can explain this evening's adventures in the morning," Minsheng said.

I instinctively held out my hand for the salamander and helped him hobble onto it.

He snuggled into my hand, then also yawned. The suckers on the bottom of his feet felt strange against my skin, but his body felt like a brick of heat. What kind of salamander was this?

Does he have a name? I asked Zephyr.

Not one in the human tongue.

I was going to ask what his name was in his native tongue, but I had a feeling it was something I wouldn't be able to say anyway.

Part of my mind began trying to think of suitable salamander names, but I was just too tired. That would have to wait until the morning as well.

As soon as I got the small creature upstairs, I fashioned a bed for him out of a cardigan. He curled up on top of it after turning in a couple of circles, then let out a soft roar.

Feeling more than a little pleased with myself, I got into bed, but despite my exhaustion and the long day I'd had, I couldn't fall asleep. We'd taken a big risk today, but I just couldn't let the agency take the salamander.

Finding out he was a baby separated from his family made me even more sure I'd done the right thing. But I couldn't help but wonder if the agency would work out that I'd been involved. I didn't want to put Zephyr or Minsheng and his family in danger.

Unable to sleep but with my two companions already snoring, I crept out of bed and headed to the training room. I kept the small transceiver that was connected to a bug in the agency head's room in there.

Wondering what the head of the agency had been up to

lately, I switched it on to listen to things in real-time and waited to see if Ms. Crawley was even in. By now it was five in the morning, but she'd been there when I'd attacked the agency at midnight, and the transceiver had picked up on many conversations at unconventional times. I had a feeling she worked whenever she needed to.

But if she was there now, her office was quiet. Pulling up the display, I looked for previous conversations. There was a spike of activity at about the time the salamander was on the beach. I got the machine to play back that conversation.

"I don't care how late it is. There are reports of a strange creature on the beach that started a fire—a lizard of sorts. You are going to go catch it," Crawley said.

There was silence, whoever was responding apparently not in the room. I imagined the woman on the phone having called someone and woken them up.

"I've had the details forwarded to you. There are several natives in the vicinity, and it's important they suspect nothing. Use a cover story. Suggest it's endangered or something and you're there to collect it and return it to the zoo."

She sounded more than a little irritable, no doubt wishing they would think for themselves. It made me feel a little better. They didn't know it had been a salamander, and the lack of activity on the transceiver afterward made it clear the agents hadn't yet reported in.

Feeling a little safer and more confident we'd done the right thing, I went back to bed. Hopefully we would be able to return him to his family in the morning.

CHAPTER FOUR

"What were you thinking?" Minsheng asked as I finished telling him what had happened the night before.

"I couldn't let them catch it. It's a helpless creature, and who knows what they'd have done with it?"

Minsheng sighed and threw his hands up.

"I know. I'd have done the same thing in that regard. But I'm not the one who promised the agency I wouldn't get involved so they'd leave me alone."

"No," I replied, sitting down. But I knew, looking at Zephyr and seeing the small nod he gave me, that he approved of my decision. I had done the right thing in everyone's mind.

"I guess we'd better help find his family, and you had better continue training. If you have pissed off the agency, you'll need to defend yourself again."

"And you and the others," I replied. If we had made a mess of it, I didn't want them to suffer for it. The restaurant had been trashed once and had to close for the better part of a week. I didn't want a repeat of that.

I expected Minsheng to try to talk to the salamander about where he had come from and where his family might be. Instead he called Chris and asked his friend if there had been any sightings of fire salamanders in the area.

I tried to ignore the conversation and concentrate on my training. After the fiasco at the beach last night, I was more than ready to be able to fly. With this in mind, I went back to my platform once more and pulled in as much energy as I could.

After taking several deep breaths to try to calm myself and prepare for a fall, I pushed the air out through my hands. More than a little nervous, I overcooked it. I rose into the air and began somersaulting.

Out of control, I stopped pushing out air and tried to find a way not to crash. I continued somersaulting for a moment longer before gravity took over and I hit the edge of the mat.

"That was close," I said as I got to my feet.

"I'll fetch more mats," Minsheng replied, still on the phone to Chris.

Any tips? I asked Zephyr. The dragon was lying near the door watching the salamander as he tried to slowly walk.

Do it more carefully, he replied.

I rolled my eyes. I was doing it as carefully as I could.

Trying not to let the frustration get to me, I climbed back up and tried again. This time I managed to hover above the platform for about a second.

"You're doing it," Minsheng said as he came back with another mat.

I looked at him, and the simple movement of my head overbalanced me. Wobbling, I came off the front of the platform. As I tried to compensate for the forward momentum while panicking in case I overshot the mats again, I rose higher and smacked into the roof.

Stunned, I fell and hit the mat with an almighty bang, my whole body throbbing.

"Ouch," I said a moment later, not wanting to move.

"Sorry," Minsheng said, finally putting down the mat he held.

Sighing, I pushed to my feet. Why couldn't I get this? So many of the other techniques and applications Minsheng had tried to teach me seemed to have come naturally, but there was something about this. I just couldn't wrap my head around the gentle sort of controls I needed.

I was still trying and still failing when Chris arrived an hour later. As he walked into the training room he watched me, not speaking to anyone as he chewed gum.

Only after I crash-landed once again, this time barely making it off the platform before one hand gave way and I toppled sideways, did he comment.

"Are you trying to jet air from your hands to propel yourself?" Chris asked. "Like a superhero?"

"Something like that," I replied.

"He does it from his feet as well. The four points of control make it easier."

I stopped, blinking. Was it as simple as that? Did I just need more points of control? Before I could even think about trying it, Chris walked over to Minsheng and slapped something on the table.

More than a little curious, I walked over to see what it was. I wasn't the only one who was looking at it like it was strange.

"This acts as a heat detector. It's connected to a bunch of automatically reporting weather stations around the city. You'd be surprised how many amateurs like to measure this, that, and the other." Chris turned it on.

A map of the area going in each direction for about five blocks popped up on the screen.

"Can it zoom out? I asked.

"Sadly, no. I threw this together from some other little gadgets I had. If I'd had another couple of weeks, I could have made you something much fancier."

"You made that in an hour?"

"About that. As I said, I cobbled it together from other gadgets I had lying around. The hard part was making everything I needed fit in this box."

Minsheng picked it up and pressed a few buttons, getting it to activate.

"How does it work?" Minsheng asked a moment later.

"It's not perfect, but it should detect pockets of heat when a family of salamanders gets too close." Chris reached over and pressed a few more buttons.

"But it's not picking up on the salamander we have. Newton isn't making it register any heat differences," I said, looking at the screen over Minsheng's shoulder.

"He's only one little salamander," Chris replied. "Alone and as small as he is, he can't make enough of a difference in the air temperature for a weather station on a roof to pick up on it."

"We are looking for the whole family. There will be at least three of them, and if my notes on fire salamanders are correct, the father will be the size of a raccoon." Minsheng smiled.

I blinked, wondering what book Minsheng had looked up the salamander in. It was as if he had read my mind. He went over to the bookshelves, reached for a large volume near the top, and brought it over to the table. Putting it down, he flicked through the pages until he found one with a picture that looked like Newton.

"Oh, look," I said. "It's Newton."

"Newton?" Chris asked.

"Yeah, like Newt. But better." I grinned.

"What's wrong with Salamander?"

"Salamander is not a name. He needed a name, and Zephyr assured me I couldn't say his real one."

"Zephyr talks now?" Chris asked, looking at the dragon.

"In my head," I said. "At least, I think that's what I'm hearing."

Chris and Minsheng chuckled and I thought Zephyr did the same, a faint rumble coming from his direction.

I like Newton. Zephyr's words made it clear he'd been listening to the conversation.

We can't keep him. He needs to go back to his family.

I know. But for now, he's cute.

Very. And he'd make a great hot water bottle. We still can't keep him.

As I finished thinking this, I smiled and shook my head. When had I become the responsible one?

While Chris showed Minsheng how the device worked and they talked about all sorts of other things, from how the restaurant was doing to the latest information on something in the newspapers, I tried to refocus on my training.

I wanted to try the trick Chris had suggested, of using

all four of my limbs to control my flight and see if it made any difference. But I'd never considered using my feet at all before. A few times I'd made strikes in combat more powerful by adding a push from the air to them, but I'd never formed more constant jets of wind from anywhere but my hands.

Still standing on the floor, I tried to imagine how that might feel and what that might look like. I'd already crashed into the ceiling once today, and I didn't want to do it again if this went wrong.

Putting my hands down by my sides, I drew in the air and energy I would want to push out and then concentrated on dialing it up slowly.

At first, very little happened. I wasn't used to using my feet in any part of my magic. While it had come fairly naturally to manipulate it with my hands and imagine what I wanted to happen, using my feet had not occurred to me.

Maybe I should have watched more superhero movies because I soon knocked myself off my feet, tumbling onto the mat.

Getting up again, I took a deep breath, closed my eyes for a moment, and tried to imagine what it was I wanted to do. Keeping that picture in my head, I drew in the air around me and then pushed it outward.

This time I used all four of my limbs together, trying to match the outward thrust and keep my body rigid. As I lifted off the ground, I wobbled and landed again after losing concentration as I began to panic.

It was progress, however, and a lot more controlled than my previous attempts. Focusing on my breathing and keeping it calm, I repeated the process for the third time.

As the pressure grew beneath my feet and I used my hands to steady myself, I lifted off the ground. For a moment I hovered, doing my best to keep calm despite the excitement now building inside me.

I heard and saw Zephyr get up and slowly come closer out of the corner of my eye. Carefully I applied more pressure, trying to lift higher. Bit by bit I rose, and this time as I wobbled, I managed to rebalance myself with my hands.

When I was about two feet off the ground, I tried to move forward by leaning that way slightly and moving my hands to help keep me balanced. Once again, I overcompensated and sent myself tumbling to the ground.

For a moment I lay there, cushioned by the mat, feeling like I might finally be making some progress. I may not have flown in any particular direction, but I had managed to hover, and it had been controlled for at least a few seconds. It was also a lot easier when I had four points of contact and air pressure instead of two.

"Do you want me to help you find the family?" Chris asked as he finished his conversation with Minsheng.

Minsheng shook his head and glanced at me.

"I'm sure we can go as soon as it's dark," I replied. "Zephyr will be able to come with us then, and he can communicate with Newton."

Chris shrugged, gathered the rest of his things, and headed back to his car.

I groaned as I saw the clock. It was time for my shift in the restaurant.

"I'd best get changed," I said, not really wanting to. If I was being truthful, I wanted nothing more than to keep trying to fly. But for today I'd run out of time.

"I'll keep an eye on Newton and Zephyr. I am also going to message the organization again. We really need a bigger training room. Especially if you and Zephyr are going to be flying together."

Minsheng's confidence in my abilities put a smile on my face as I walked out of the room. The first time we'd come down to the training room, we'd come by a convoluted route, heading up into the attic and then down a secret trap door.

Zephyr was far too big for that now, so instead, we had to come and go via the double back doors that opened into a small garden. From there, Zephyr could get to the garage and through the now-much-wider doorway to the kitchen.

Of course, he couldn't do any of that while it was light. Too many windows from the surrounding buildings could see into the garden.

That meant I had to leave him there. Thankfully, he wasn't far from me while I was waitressing, and Minsheng regularly stayed with him.

It wasn't ideal, and already a lot of doorways had had to be widened. So far the organization was paying for it, and apparently, they were looking for somewhere better. But premises in LA that were for sale or came with a long enough lease were hard to find and cost an awful lot. The organization seemed to be dragging its heels.

Although they had sent me a gift and Minsheng worked for them, I didn't think much of this organization. Not one of them had come to meet me, and they clearly didn't understand our needs.

As I arrived at the kitchen, Daisy handed me an apron and the small device the restaurant used to take orders.

I fixed the usual waitressing smile to my face and took them from her. Hopefully it would be an easy shift. As soon as it was done, I intended to get back to my practice.

I was going to fly. I also wanted to help Newton find his family.

CHAPTER FIVE

I didn't know if it was the different clientele or because my employers were people I got along with so well, but I enjoyed waitressing at the restaurant far more than I ever had at any of the diners in the past.

Most of the tables were full of families. It was clear many were tourists, but some were people who lived nearby. There were very few lecherous men, and even when there was a stag party, they were far more polite.

The evening grew later in a rush of orders, moving plates, and drinks. The restaurant was packed, the tourists unaware of what had happened in the restaurant eight weeks earlier, and the regulars having forgotten about it.

I hadn't forgotten about it, however. It was one of the reasons I'd offered to work there. Even though they were paying me, I felt like I was helping them in return.

As the restaurant grew quieter and I found a table to sit down and grab some dinner, I finally took a moment to look around. This place was starting to feel like it could be home, a home I'd never had before.

There was a warmth to Minsheng's family I'd only ever seen in films. To be part of it and welcomed into it regularly blew me away.

I had just finished eating and put my chopsticks down when several cars pulled up outside. Instantly, I got to my feet. One glance at the array of matching sedans confirmed my worst fears. The agency was here.

My blood ran cold. Had they come for Zephyr and me, or just the fire salamander?

As the first two agents got out of the car and came toward the door, I moved toward them.

While I did, I reached out for Zephyr with my mind, hoping he would be listening.

We've got company, I sent.

On my way, he replied.

Around me, the other two waitresses gently encouraged the few remaining customers to leave.

I stopped on my side of the little entry podium and drew in the air around me. While I was doing this, six agents came inside. Despite all of them wearing sunglasses in the late evening, I knew one of them was looking straight at me.

"You're not welcome here," I said. "Please leave."

"'Fraid I can't do that," the lead agent replied.

For a moment there was silence as the agents let the customers who had just paid walk out the door.

As soon as the restaurant was empty of everyone but staff and agents, the lead agent looked my way again. He seemed to sneer, and I could imagine his eyes moving up and down as he took me in.

A part of me longed to send him flying and wipe that

look off his face. Instead, I gave him my politest, most fake smile.

"As you can see, we are now closed. It's very much time you left."

"I'm not going anywhere until you hand over the two fugitives you have." He folded his arms across his chest, the muscles bulging.

I resisted the temptation to lift something large and heavy and have it float near me as if I were going to throw it at him. This wasn't a pissing contest.

"Then I'm afraid you're going to be very disappointed. There aren't any fugitives here," I replied instead.

"My information indicates you have a juvenile fire sala-mander and an adolescent dragon. Both are to be handed over at once."

"Your information is wrong. We all know I bonded with a dragon. The dragon and I kicked your asses only two months ago. After a little discussion with your boss, it was agreed that Zephyr and I were to be left alone. That bargain still stands." But even as I said this, I knew we had interfered, and I didn't believe it was a coincidence that the agents were here now when they could have visited any time before today.

"I strongly suggest you don't fight us this time. You aren't going to like how this ends. Now, you've had your fun. Hand over the dragon and the fire salamander and no one gets hurt."

"No," I said. "You're not getting my dragon or anything else under my protection in this building, even if I have no idea what you mean by 'fire salamander.'"

"No point in being coy. We saw you and the dragon in

the parking lot surveillance footage from the beach. It's all the proof we need. If you don't hand them over, I'll have no choice but to use force." He grinned as he finished speaking, making it clear that using force was just what he wanted to do.

I no longer held back, knowing this was only going to go one way. All the air I had been sucking in since the beginning of the conversation I now propelled forward, aiming for all of the agents. It hit them head-on, knocking two of them off their feet and pushing the others back even though they'd braced themselves.

Before anyone could do anything else, four more agents ran in. Each of them held a strange shield-like device. At the same time, the agents inside tried to get to their feet again and reached for weapons.

As Zephyr and Minsheng hurried into the room from the kitchen, I dropped back a little. It would give the agents time to gather themselves, but it would also mean I wasn't trying to hold ten of them back alone.

Together, the three of us formed a line, Minsheng carrying one of the tranquilizer guns from an earlier encounter with the agents. As the nearest two agents pulled similar-looking guns out, I blasted them with air again. This time I used more precision to hit the muzzles of the guns from underneath and lift up.

Both of the agents' weapons fired toward the ceiling, and feathered darts stuck out of the tiles a fraction of a second later.

Zephyr took a few steps forward, opened his mouth, and exhaled. Before the nearest agent to him could get back, the man inhaled the gas and grew rigid before toppling over. The rest of the agents quickly donned masks, however, and I gulped in surprise.

Masks were going to make this fight much harder.

Focused on using short blasts of wind to interfere with their aim and a steadier breeze to blow more of Zephyr's paralyzing vapor toward them, I didn't notice what was going on until too late. An agent near the back pulled out what looked like a grenade launcher. A large net came hurtling out of it and landed on Zephyr, trapping him.

I growled my fury along with him as I rushed to his side and tried to pull it off. There was no way I was going to let him be taken. The net seemed to be designed to tangle, however, and in Zephyr's panic and my fear, I couldn't get it off.

The next shots from the agents' darts hit Zephyr. They'd previously been strong enough to knock him out like a light, but he was far bigger now. Two hits made him woozy, however. Fear wrapping icy tendrils around my heart, I rushed in front of him, hurling all the wind I could at the group of agents. The men behind the shields held, but the rest were pushed back, along with most of the furniture on their side of the restaurant.

I heard Minsheng shout to someone behind me, "Get a knife. We need to cut him loose." It sounded like Daisy replied, but I didn't look to check. I wasn't taking my attention off the agents again. If they wanted to get to Zephyr or the salamander, I was going to make them go through me.

However, I couldn't use magic like this forever. The

sustained powerful jet was draining me fast, and the shielded men were barely affected. They now crouched, guns in hands and masks on.

They shot at me some more, but their darts went wide. I could only hope they didn't hit Minsheng or his family and trust they were trying to cut Zephyr loose.

Hold on, buddy, I sent. *We'll get you out and safe.*

At the same time, I stopped the jet of air against the shields. One fell forward, having been pushing so hard against my airstream that he couldn't stop himself once the counterforce was removed.

Minsheng shot him, getting him in the arm with a dart. The agent didn't get up again. That left us with six. As soon as my blast of air stopped, the agents recovered and continued shooting at us.

I had no choice but to jet air again to keep any darts from hitting Minsheng and me—or Zephyr; one more hit could put him to sleep. It helped a little, but a dart hit Minsheng's sister as she came around the side to try to help pull off the net she'd been cutting.

She gasped, slowly fell into a deep sleep, and toppled over.

"Pull back," Minsheng called as he and another member of his family rushed to Daisy's side.

"Get Zephyr out from under that net and then we can do so," I half-said and half-growled as I blasted air at more darts to knock them off-course.

We needed a better way to shield ourselves, and we needed it now.

My eyes fixed on the shields the agents held. Four of

the six remaining men were huddled behind them, shooting as they could. I studied the angles for a moment. They appeared to have been designed to spread any airflow directed at them and enable the person behind it to push forward or hold their ground.

But a shield on the floor with an agent not far from it, trying to reach for it and use it to protect himself, showed me the underside. They were just as curved on the inside, which meant I could hit them from the other side with great effect.

As the agent's fingers found purchase on a strap attached to the inside, I pulled air down and toward it, catching the dome and pulling it toward me. He and the unconscious agent who had originally held it came hurtling toward me with the shield, dragged across the floor.

As Minsheng picked up Daisy's knife to continue cutting Zephyr free, her body now safely out of view, he kicked something over to me. It was a large pepper grinder offered to customers with their meals. I grabbed it, and as the shield and agents arrived in front of me, I knelt and brought it down on the head of the conscious one.

It connected with him so hard the grinder broke and spilled pepper all over his hair. I yanked the shield out from under him and the original wearer as he yelled, the pepper getting in his eyes, mouth, and nose.

As I lifted the shield and stood again, I was amazed at how light it felt. A dart *thunked* into it before falling to the floor, the other agents' guns now all trained on me.

"Zephyr's free," Minsheng called. "Fall back."

Gritting my teeth and more than a little tired, I nodded, but I didn't back up. Instead, I drew in all the air I could again and hurled it forward, retreating one step at a time.

Only when I was within a few feet of the door did I turn and hurry back, dropping the blast of wind a fraction of a second later. Someone slammed the door behind me.

My eyes were drawn to Zephyr. The dragon was clearly still woozy as he wobbled by the garage door. Minsheng had an arm over his shoulders, helping to guide him.

While we stood there, more cars pulled up and more agents got out, yelling at their comrades.

Shitsticks.

Quite, Zephyr's voice replied, sounding deeper and less focused than normal.

When six more agents got out, all of them with shields and gas masks, I frowned. This fight had just gone from hard to practically impossible. We should have been managing better than this, but I'd never faced so many of them at once. And they were far better equipped than the last time.

One of the newcomers strode up to the building, his head higher and his suit dark gray rather than black. He also wore no sunglasses. Was this another leader? I had no way of knowing, but the agent who'd demanded I hand over Zephyr and Newton left the restaurant briefly to talk to him. They conferred for a few seconds before all of them came inside again.

"You should get your family somewhere safer," I said to Minsheng, looking back to see him and his uncle still there. Daisy had evidently been taken somewhere else.

"Most of them are already gone," Minsheng replied. "We should go too."

I bit my lip, not wanting to flee.

"Not yet," I said. "If we just run now, they'll think they can best us any time. We've got to hit them harder first. Take more of them out."

"How do you propose we do that?" he asked, clearly unimpressed by the idea. "Zephyr can't take another dart, and you probably can't take one anymore."

Zephyr's voice rang in my head. *But you still have one of their shields. And if you can buy me some more time, I feel stronger and my head is more clear with each passing minute.*

"I want to draw them to the training room. Minsheng, please go get Newton and take him somewhere safer. Zephyr and I will do the rest."

Minsheng looked like he might argue with me for a moment, but eventually he nodded. He swept toward the training room. Then I looked at his uncle.

"When I give the word, open the door and then get out of here as well. We're going to be retreating in a hurry."

He nodded and went to pull out the mop handle they'd shoved through the kitchen door handle to keep it closed. It rattled a little, letting the men in the other room know something was coming, so I hung back.

Ready? I asked Zephyr.

As ready as possible, but I'd prefer a little longer.

You and me both, buddy.

I took a moment to suck in the air and strode through the door, the shield raised. I only glanced over it for a moment before I jettisoned the wind in as powerful a stroke as I could muster. With most of the agents behind similar shields, it barely had an effect, but I hadn't been aiming for them.

Feeling a little guilty that I was trashing the restaurant even more spectacularly than I had the first time, I caught all the tables and chairs and flung them at the agents. Although the shields protected them to some degree, the double onslaught as wooden furniture cracked, splintered, and hurtled toward them was enough to knock most of them off their feet.

That's about as much time as I can buy, I told Zephyr as I began to back up.

Okay. But you're going to want to hold your breath.

I was about to ask what he meant, but instead I glanced at the kitchen. It was full of a dense white cloud, no doubt the paralyzing gas he created.

Glad I had warning and knew the way through the kitchen, I sucked in a final lungful of fresh air and dived into the fog. At first I was overwhelmed by fear, unable to see the shield I carried, but my feet carried me through the haze toward the garage and I slipped inside. The area was clear and Zephyr lingered by the door to the back garden.

I fell back to join him, grateful for the fresh air by the open door.

You know most of them can come through that fine, right? They're wearing gas masks.

Most of them. It will still make it harder for them to follow. If they move slowly, it's concentrated enough it can seep in through their skin slowly.

And you didn't think to mention that before I went through it?

You didn't linger. And your elven blood processes it quicker than a human anyway, just like the tranquilizers.

Rolling my eyes, I checked to see if the garden was clear. So far, no agents had come this way to try to sneak up on us from behind. We hurried to the training room, heading down the short flight of stairs. It was time to prepare a few surprises for the agents.

CHAPTER SIX

As soon as Zephyr and I were in the training room, I rushed over to the rack of martial arts weapons and selected a nunchuck I was familiar with. With that in one hand and the shield in the other, I moved to the edge of the maze-like training section. When it wasn't switched on, it was just a maze of corridors, doors, and openings—the perfect hiding place for someone who knew it well to be able to confuse and attack those who didn't.

Leaving my weapon and shield at one end and looking for more of the obstacles Minsheng sometimes used in it, I also noticed there was another dart gun on a shelf by the door. I grabbed it and motioned for Zephyr to stay put. I wasn't about to waste a good opportunity to shoot at easy targets.

Heading back through the garden, I paused by the open garage door. I could hear clattering from the kitchen, but it was clear none of the agents had made it through the fog yet. The door from the kitchen to the garage was obscured,

55

the gas cloud Zephyr had created beginning to spill out into the garage. I held the gun trained on it.

For a few minutes, I stood waiting. I began to wonder if anyone was going to come out. Eventually, someone emerged from the gas, walking at an angle, their shield not protecting them from attack from my direction. Without hesitating, I fired. The dart hit him in the side, and he went down like a sack of potatoes.

The next agent tripped over him, shields and bodies making a loud clatter. I shot him as well, and the agent never managed to get back to his feet.

After that, the following agents were more cautious. They edged out, testing with their feet. Working in pairs, they were shielded, and only their heads poked above.

I shot at them anyway. Two darts went wide, but I managed to hit one in the neck. Out of darts, I threw the gun at the remaining agent a fraction of a second after his partner collapsed and took his shield with him. The gun caught him on the arm, but I don't know if it did anything more than make him angry.

Not waiting around to find out, I legged it to the training room.

As I came in the door, I noticed Zephyr up on the platform closest to this end of the room. His eyes were trained on the doorway as if he were about to attack. I finished my preparations, stacking some boxes and setting up a couple of the tripwires and traps Minsheng liked to use sometimes.

Finally, I grabbed the transceiver off the shelf and shot a glance at the bookshelf. Some of the books were gone, no doubt grabbed by Minsheng as he came to get Newton, but

I knew it was going to break his heart to leave the rest behind. I had to do something.

Grabbing a nearby bag, I tucked in the books I thought were most precious and important, then ran with the bag to the secret staircase at the other end and took the route up to the attic. I stowed it inside, desperately hoping no one would stumble upon it by accident, then I shut the hatch and made sure it wasn't visible, dragging a weapon rack over it just in case.

With that done, I went back to my shield and nunchuck, placed myself at the end of the maze, and waited. Once I was out of the way of the door, Zephyr exhaled again, sending a large plume of gas toward it.

It was only a little hazy by the time a figure appeared. With no idea how many agents were left, I waited until I'd drawn their attention. As I pulled back into the maze, Zephyr let out a loud roar and flew over my head to drop into the maze behind me.

I waited, the nunchuck and shield ready for whoever rushed around the corner first. As I stood there, I listened to the sounds of running feet. Some of the agents clearly ran to other entrances of the maze. For now I wasn't worried. I would hear any agents coming from the other directions, and Zephyr had my back.

The second an agent rounded the corner and appeared in front of me, I lashed out. I caught him on the side with the nunchuck, pulling it back and hitting him a second time before he knew what had happened.

Pushing forward with his shield, he tried to ram me. I dodged to one side while pulling as much air as I could toward me and to the other side. It caught in his shield, ripping it from his grasp.

Again I struck with the nunchuck, hammering blows on him. He managed to block some of them, but I was too fast for him to block them all or stand a chance of recovering enough to attack back. I was now so used to using my elemental magic to speed up my attacks that I was doing it without thinking.

Only when a second agent appeared did I relent. I mimicked the attack the first agent had used on me and hurled myself into both of them with my shield.

The nearest one toppled into the agent behind him, knocking them both down. I almost overbalanced as well, catching myself with jets of air from my hands and pushing myself back up.

Grabbing the second shield, I ran farther into the maze after Zephyr. Going left and then right, we instinctively headed toward the sound of an agent tripping one of the traps.

We rounded a corner to find an agent buried under fake rubble. It wasn't as heavy as real debris, but Minsheng had been getting me to train my defensive capabilities, and normally I would have held the containers up with nothing but air.

I hopped over the unmoving agent. As there was more noise and more traps were set off, I knew it was time to get out of there.

Take the next exit, I sent to Zephyr.

Before he could reply, another agent appeared, the only one without sunglasses—Mr. In Charge. Zephyr stopped, and I hurried to his side.

I expected the agent to attack, but he merely paused and looked at us.

"You must be Aella-Faye," he said. Without waiting for an acknowledgment, he looked at Zephyr. "And the dragon you've decided to protect."

"His name is Zephyr." I took a step closer, twirling the nunchuck.

"And the salamander?" he asked.

"Not here," I replied, pulling in air and holding onto it. "But even if it were, I wouldn't be handing it to you."

"She said you were stubborn."

"Did she also tell you we had an agreement?"

"Eventually. Of course, you've broken that agreement."

"I'm pretty sure you're the kind of person who wouldn't have respected it anyway."

"True. I'd never have made the agreement." He pulled a gun from his pocket as he spoke, aiming it at me. "Now, I really must insist you come with me."

I didn't reply, instead unleashing all the air I'd been holding in one jet at the gun and his head. He fired, but the shot went high. I didn't wait to find out if he was using bullets or tranquilizer darts.

I charged at him, still pumping air out in concentrated bursts.

As I got closer, I used my nunchuck to smack the gun out of his hands. He fell into a defensive pose, making it clear he also knew a martial art. I didn't hesitate to go on the offensive and try to hit him with the nunchuck anywhere that was exposed.

After so much fighting, my body was beginning to tire, and I found I couldn't concentrate or draw enough energy to control the air around me and speed up my attacks very much. Far more evenly matched than I'd have liked, Mr. In Charge blocked several lunges and kicked at me. I managed to dodge, almost falling over Zephyr's tail.

Not long after, another agent appeared behind us. Zephyr turned and bit the agent's shield, engaging in an elaborate game of tug-of-war.

I only had a moment to take in the new situation before Mr. In Charge grabbed my arm, attempting to get me down on the floor and pin me. I spun out of the attack by using his momentum against him and smacked him into the wall. For a moment he was stunned, but he quickly recovered and rounded on me again.

We needed to get out of here since no doubt more agents were on the way, but I couldn't find a quick way to best the agent in front of me, not when I was out of energy and my body was exhausted.

As Mr. In Charge attacked again, I blocked with the nunchuck, attempting to wrap it around his wrist and take control of that arm.

The agent was too fast and got out of my grasp. He backed up, sliding to one side so he was no longer against the wall, and blocked my exit once more. I growled as I rushed toward him, determined to fight my way out of this.

But as quickly as I attacked, he blocked and defended. I couldn't get out.

From behind, I could hear Zephyr making muffled roaring noises, his mouth no doubt still locked on something. More than once I tried to check on him, but I couldn't take my eyes off the agent in front of me to see how he was faring.

Just as I was beginning to consider surrendering and trying to escape before they could lock us up somewhere, a friendly face appeared behind Mr. In Charge.

Minsheng fired, and a tranquilizer dart hit Mr. In Charge in the back. His eyes went wide before the sedative took effect and he hit the deck. I rushed to Zephyr's aid.

Using the last of the air I had the energy to control, I blasted the agent no longer protected by his shield and sent him flying into the wall. His head hit it hard, and he slumped like a rag doll.

Zephyr spat out the shield. We ran to Minsheng's side, then all three of us were hurrying out the side of the maze.

"Not that way," Minsheng said as I went to run out the back doors. "There are more agents there now."

Instead, Minsheng hurried toward the secret staircase to the attic. We didn't argue, but I glanced to the shelves to note that more of the books and belongings were gone.

"Chris helped," Minsheng said. "And we found the bag you packed. Thank you for that."

I nodded, not replying as Zephyr halted at the door. He might have fit through the staircase before, but he was far too big now.

I stopped, deciding that I'd just have to face the agents. There was no way I was leaving him.

Go that way, Zephyr sent into my head. *Get the car ready nearby and let me know where.*

I'm not leaving you.

I'm not asking you to. I'll gas this lot so badly they won't know where I am and then fly out, but I can't do that while you're here.

Minsheng grabbed my arm and tried to pull me away, but I resisted. There was no way I was letting Zephyr out of my sight if I could help it.

You tell me immediately if something goes wrong.

Only after he nodded did I turn, seeing Minsheng pick up the bag of books I'd left and hurry up the stairs. I followed, my legs protesting at the climb after all the running around.

Thankfully, the route was still familiar, and we were quickly down on the second floor again, coming out not far from my bedroom. I darted in and grabbed my bag, shoving in my phone, some clothes, and the box I kept the broken pieces of Zephyr's egg in. I also grabbed the ornate basket I'd found the egg in. I'd gone back to my old apartment to get it after our little truce had gotten the agents to back off and leave it unwatched.

You okay? I asked Zephyr, feeling him get farther away as Minsheng and I hurried down the main staircase and into the private area on the bottom floor.

For now. But there are a lot of agents, and they have gas masks. I think one of them might have another of those net launchers too.

Shitsticks.

That is an accurate description.

I almost laughed, having meant to describe the situation, not the launcher. However, knowing Zephyr was in danger made up my mind.

"Here, take these to the car for me and bring it as close

as you dare. Zephyr's in trouble." I thrust my stuff at Minsheng, not giving him a choice.

I ran through to the kitchen, finding it almost clear with two agents on the floor, wearing gas masks but out cold. I yanked the gas mask off the nearest agent, and Minsheng, who'd come back in, helped me strap it on.

The claustrophobic feeling it gave me was intense until I felt a strange tug to the pit of my stomach.

Zephyr? What happened?

Another net, and something else. Not sure what it is. It hurts.

On my way.

No, this place is full of gas now.

Coming anyway. I've got a mask. I grabbed a knife from the kitchen and ran back upstairs. Fear gripped my heart and the danger to Zephyr gnawed at my stomach until I could do nothing but hurry to his side.

I took the stairs two at a time, slamming my hand on the button to open the wall and let me through. I was met by a dense white swirling fog, only the outlines of shapes visible here and there.

Slamming into the first agent I saw, I knocked him off his feet and didn't hesitate to grab his mask and yank it off. The agent had the sense to hold his breath and tried to grab at me to unmask me as well. I darted to one side and kicked him in the stomach. It knocked the air out of him, and his instincts had him inhale before he could stop himself.

He collapsed.

Where are you?

Far-left corner. Was that you making all the commotion?

Probably.

I got to my feet and ran his way, more than a little relieved when I saw he was trapped in a net but huddled in the back corner. I went to grab it to cut it off but got zapped.

It's a fucking electric net.

It doesn't do that painful tingling thing if I keep it on just my back scales and the rest of my body away from it.

That doesn't help me, but it's good to know.

I needed something that didn't conduct electricity to wrap around my hand. Thinking fast, I dashed over to the martial arts equipment and yanked on one of the sparring gloves. It was made of plastic, padding, and elastic. Not perfect, but it should help.

Running back, I spotted another agent, but I could do nothing but smack him with my padded left hook. He turned a gun on me, but it was clear he couldn't see me properly. I ducked as he fired and then powered up, pushing off the floor to thump him under the chin. Despite the padding, it knocked him off his feet.

He dropped the gun, and it clattered and skittered across the floor to me. Momentarily putting the knife down, I picked up the gun. I shot at the agent's leg, worried it carried real bullets. Thankfully it was another tranquilizer gun, so feathers stuck out of his calf.

I stuffed the gun in a pocket and picked the knife up again.

No one else got in my way as I returned to Zephyr's side. As I knelt beside him and started to cut away the net, I noticed my limbs beginning to get stiff. Was Zephyr's paralyzing gas starting to hurt me too?

I tried not to think about it but cut the netting as

quickly as I could, grateful the chef's knives were always super-sharp. As soon as the cut was wide enough, I yanked it off him and set him free.

We ran for the door. I ripped off the glove, dropping it and switching the knife to that hand. Then I drew the gun again. My fingers struggled to bend around it; I was definitely growing stiffer.

I need to get out of this fog, Zephyr.

I don't doubt it. I'm impressed you've lasted this long.

I rolled my eyes at his response. If we hadn't been in so much danger, I'd have been cross that he hadn't warned me. Well, in his own way, he had.

As we neared the door, I saw two more agents in a rigid heap. It seemed I'd lasted far longer than they had.

The second we get out the doors, get into the air, I told Zephyr.

What will you do?

Run.

That's not a very good plan.

Got a better one? As I asked the question, we burst into the light, almost blinded since the air was clearer. I spotted three agents huddled behind shields and more stood by cars.

Before I could even think of running, Zephyr launched into the air above me and grabbed my shoulders with his front claws. They dug in painfully, but he lifted me into the air with him, carrying us to one side and above the wall to our right.

As soon as we were on the other side, he dropped me. I tried to bend my knees and roll, but it was badly timed. I ended up crouched and fell on my side instead. Pain flared, but I did my best to ignore it.

Zephyr flew on as I scrambled to my feet. I could hear shots, but I ran after him, not sure if they were aiming at him or me. We both darted around the next corner, then I spotted the large van Minsheng had rescued us in before. We hurried toward it, Zephyr beating me, landing, and tumbling into it while I was still twenty yards away.

"Hurry," Minsheng called, his eyes going wide as he looked over my shoulder.

I tried to find more speed as I sprinted toward the truck, but I was still a few yards away when I heard a shot and felt the familiar sting when a dart hit my back.

Stumbling forward, I forced my legs to keep running and used my hands to steady my wobbly body and jet me toward the van. It sort of worked, and Minsheng caught me when my legs gave out. He hauled me into the back of the van as someone else pulled the doors shut behind us.

Slowly, fighting it every inch of the way, I slipped into oblivion.

CHAPTER SEVEN

As I came to, I could hear two people talking but not what they said. For a moment I kept my eyes closed, cozy and warm while we drove along. The memories of what had happened before I'd been put to sleep came to mind, making me feel even less like showing I was awake.

Now I had time to think about it, I was angry at myself. Angry about the risks we'd taken and angry about how much Minsheng and his family had just lost to protect me, Zephyr, and Newton.

I can tell you're awake, Zephyr said in my head.

Really? I still didn't open my eyes.

Yes. Your breathing changes subtly, but also, I just know. You're suddenly there in my mind.

I knew what Zephyr meant, but I didn't know how to explain it either. Since I'd put on Tuviel's necklace, I'd been aware of Zephyr in a way I hadn't been before. It definitely enhanced the bond between us.

When the voices in the background faded, I opened my eyes, spotted Minsheng, and took stock of where I was. We were still in the back of Chris' van. My jacket was folded under my head and I was lying next to Zephyr, his warm body pressed against my back.

It looked like Minsheng's books had been separated into a few different bags, Daisy and Chris now carried some of them as well. Newton was lying on my cardigan in front of me.

He peered at me and croaked when he saw I was awake. That drew Minsheng's attention. He turned to look at me, and I saw his sister Daisy sitting beyond him in the passenger seat beside Chris.

"I'm so sorry," I said, feeling a familiar wave of guilt. "Your poor restaurant."

"It's not your fault, Aella. As I said last time. But I think it will be some time before any of us can return." Minsheng looked down and away, hiding the sadness I knew would be there.

"I broke my promise." I looked at Newton since rescuing the little guy must have been the trigger.

"You rescued someone who needed it." Minsheng reached out and stroked Newton's head. The fire salamander leaned into it, glowing slightly.

"We'd have done the same," Daisy said. "Just like we took you and Zephyr in. We all knew the danger."

"Where is everyone else?" I asked, sitting up a little.

"They've gone to one of the other restaurants," Minsheng replied. "They'll be safe there for now. The agency will concentrate on you."

I frowned, not liking Minsheng's words in more than one way. I didn't want the others to be in danger because of me, and I didn't appreciate being hunted again.

"How long was I out?" I asked when I noticed the sun wasn't as high in the sky as I would have expected.

"Only an hour or so. Much less than I would have been had I been hit with a dart."

"Any length of time is too long," I replied.

Silence fell as I tried to think. There had to be some way to put this right or make sure the agency left me alone for good. Whoever the new person in charge was, he clearly wasn't interested in a truce. Could I change his mind, or was I going to have to remove him from the picture?

"We need to get somewhere safe." I looked at Minsheng and Chris, wondering where we were driving. "Somewhere we can make a new plan."

"That's what we're working on, but it takes a little while to get out of LA." Minsheng sighed.

"We're not leaving LA. There's got to be somewhere we can lie low until we can sort this mess out again."

"Where do you suggest?" Minsheng asked. "I don't particularly want to see another building I own trashed."

It was a good point, but my feelings were steadfast on one point. We weren't going to be run out of LA.

"Before we do anything else, I think we should try to find Newton's family and return him. He is clearly not safe with us, not long-term."

At first I thought Minsheng was going to argue with that as well, but Daisy reached out from the passenger seat and rested her hand on his arm.

"She has a point," she said. "That little guy probably just wants to get back to his parents."

Eventually, Minsheng nodded. A moment later, he

reached into the bag beside him and pulled out the device Chris had given him. He switched it on, but we were nowhere near the area of LA where Newton's family probably was.

Zephyr? I said in my head, hoping he'd hear me. *Does Newton know roughly where his parents are?*

They weren't far from the beach. Fire salamanders like being out in the sun at the end of the day to recharge so they can last through the cold night.

I nodded. It made a lot of sense. I relayed the information to Minsheng.

"The beach is the other way," he replied.

I shrugged. They were the ones who had gone in the wrong direction while I slept. While I appreciated them trying to help, it was clear they were only thinking about running away. And there was no way I was going to start running again.

At the next cross street, Chris turned around.

"I won't deny it," he said, "I was hoping we wouldn't just run. There's only so much running a person can take before they want to do something else."

No one spoke as Chris stopped. Our driver was part gnome and was clearly aware of what it was like to be different. I felt like he'd read my mind.

"I mean, it felt good attacking the agency two months ago. Especially when we won."

"Yes, it did feel good. But I think we got arrogant." Minsheng ran a hand through his hair. "We should have been preparing for them to come back."

"You had me training every day. If that's not preparing, what is?" I asked.

"We could have done more."

"I hope you're not blaming yourself after telling me not to blame myself."

Our eyes met, and I thought he might argue with me and tell me it was his fault, but eventually, he nodded and sighed.

As Chris headed back the beach, a companionable silence fell between us. We'd begun planning rather than running, and it was giving us all some comfort.

No sooner had I thought this than Chris looked in his rearview mirror, and his brow creased with worry.

"I think we might have company," he said. "There are suddenly lots of black cars."

The moment he finished speaking, a siren started and a car flashed us, clearly signaling for us to pull over.

"Don't stop," Minsheng said. "They'll take Zephyr and Aella if we give them the chance."

"I've always wanted to be in a chase," Chris replied, grinning.

"Just don't crash," I replied, noting a distinct lack of seat belts in the back of the van.

"I'll do my best."

Chris floored it, pushing the van to its top speed. More of the familiar black sedans appeared, some of them clearly trying to get ahead and cut us off.

"I think we need a new plan," Daisy said as she grabbed the oh-shit handle.

When Chris yanked the steering wheel hard to the left, I slid across the floor to the right. I'd have crashed into the side if it wasn't for Minsheng grabbing me and pinning me to the side.

Even Zephyr had to dig his claws in to keep himself from sliding back and forth. When the cardigan Newton was resting on began to move around, I scooped him up and cuddled him to me.

The warm little creature burrowed in as if he found comfort in being close to me.

With no idea what I could do, I just braced myself and hoped for the best.

"Can we lose a few of these cars?" Minsheng asked.

"We might be able to lose some of them for a while. They know the van now, though, and LA is full of cameras. We won't get away from them while we're in this." Chris turned another corner sharply as if to make his point.

He sped down the next street, weaving in and out of traffic in an attempt to get ahead.

"We're gonna have to ditch the car," I said, "and make a run for it."

"Then we're gonna need to lose them on foot." Minsheng grabbed his bag and quickly slung it on his back. I did the same with mine, needing a little help while I continued to hold Newton.

I didn't like the odds of having to run away from so many agents when we were on foot, but it was clear this wasn't going to work either.

"Take the next left," Daisy said. "I know a place we can hide if we can get there."

Chris didn't hesitate, listening to her as she gave directions. Despite that, more agents appeared ahead, closing off our route and giving us nowhere else to go. Breaking hard, Chris brought the van to a halt.

Instantly I pushed open the back door and got out. As I

found my feet, I rushed around to the passenger side and pulled out the dart gun I'd stuffed in my pocket earlier. As the first agent got out of the car, I shot him. He collapsed a fraction of a second later.

The sudden shot made Daisy duck, but I grabbed her arm and pulled her away from the van, only giving her a moment to grab her pack. Feeling rather than seeing Zephyr come with me and hoping Minsheng and Chris were doing the same, we ran toward the building to the side of us. It was a large shopping mall.

Despite it being later in the day, there were plenty of people out, and I heard screams as Zephyr came with us into the mall. Trying to ignore their reactions, I looked behind to see how many agents were following us.

As we ran past the escalators, Chris and Minsheng finally catching up, I stopped and positioned myself behind one.

"Keep going," I said. "Zephyr and I are going to make it a little harder."

Minsheng didn't argue but he didn't run either, finding another position and pulling the other gun. As soon as a group of agents ran into the mall, we both fired. Several of them went down, and there were more screams.

As we sprinted off again, Zephyr exhaled, filling the atrium with gas. I felt a little guilty that innocent people were going to be paralyzed, but the majority had darted into the shops or out of the mall.

The rest seemed to have the sense to stay away from the gas, and it slowed the agents down even further as they tried to pull on gas masks before pursuing us. Hoping this meant we could lose them, we hurried to catch up with Daisy and Chris.

The two weren't far ahead, Daisy easily visible due to the bright yellow t-shirt she was wearing. At the far end of the mall, she hurried up another escalator. As we got closer, Zephyr took flight, scaring more of the shoppers.

"It's okay. He's not going to hurt anyone," I yelled. "He's with me, and he's tame."

It wasn't quite true, and I wasn't sure how many people were listening, but it had felt like the right thing to say.

"I think you're wasting your breath," Minsheng said as everyone continued to run away from us.

He was probably right, but the panicking people made it harder for the agents to get through and easier for us to get away and to wherever we needed to go.

Daisy took a right into a large toy store, almost disappearing from view. I wondered what she was thinking. The store was a dead-end, and agents were after us.

Then I saw masses of people in costumes. They were having some kind of convention, and everyone was dressed as fantasy creatures. Here, no one was even scared of Zephyr. They clearly thought he was just another part of the display.

Score one for Daisy. We rushed over to the stalls selling costumes. Minsheng pulled money out of his pocket and quickly paid for something that would fit him. I glanced at the picture of robes that would make him look like a monk before he started opening the package.

Feeling the pressure, I spotted a top that would go with the cargo pants I was wearing and help make me look like a dragonrider.

Before I could consider what it would look like, Minsheng bought it for me. A moment later, Daisy and Chris appeared, carrying outfits of their own. Daisy even had a saddle and accessories that would disguise Zephyr a little.

I looked at the door of the shop and noticed agents appearing, but the crowds were so thick they hadn't noticed us yet. I got everyone to duck and we hurried toward the back of the shop, where we'd be even harder to find.

"We need somewhere to change and quick," I said.

"There," Daisy said and pointed. I looked where she indicated to see a photo booth.

It would be a little small for all of us, but it would have to do. Either way, Minsheng and Chris hadn't hesitated in heading toward it.

What am I supposed to do? Zephyr asked.

Blend in with the displays. I'll come back out for you in a moment.

As long as no one tries to ride me.

If they do, you can always gas them.

Because that *wouldn't draw attention.*

I grinned as we rushed past the line into the photo booth.

A couple was already in there, and they froze as we entered. I ushered them out as Chris and Minsheng changed. For Minsheng, it was a matter of pulling on the robes on top of what he already wore.

For me, it wouldn't be quite so simple. I was going to need to take my t-shirt off.

I hurried to the back of the booth and turned my back on everyone else.

Trying not to blush or think about what was happening, I quickly changed.

Only once I had the new top on did I realize how revealing it was. I was still staring at myself, aghast at what I was going to have to walk out in when Daisy shoved a wig on my head. It was a long blonde braid, darker than my usual shade but not by much.

It almost completed the look, but I didn't have time for any more finishing touches.

As we rushed back out of the booth, I apologized to the waiting people. They didn't seem impressed, but they hurried into the booth anyway. I looked around for Zephyr but couldn't see him.

I joined a group of people who had different-sized dragons with them.

Looking for any dragon, I eventually spotted Zephyr trailing behind a group of teenagers. Two of them were carrying stuffed toy versions of dragons, and one of them had theirs balanced on their shoulder. Another had a small animatronic dragon, the kind that cost a fortune and didn't work well.

I hurried over to them and fell in at the back of the group. They were clearly headed for a stall selling accessories. Once there, I bought a couple of wristbands that enhanced my dragonrider look. Barely looking at the pictures on the packages, I slapped them on my wrists.

Only then did I try to see where the agents were. I noticed two by the door of the store. Another two were walking through the stalls, clearly trying to figure out who was who.

I spotted Minsheng in his robes, then Daisy and Chris. We needed a way out of the store without drawing attention to ourselves.

When a voice came over the PA, announcing a costume parade, I grinned. Costume parades were usually held outside.

I grabbed Daisy's arm and steered her toward it, grateful when she got the hint and grabbed her brother's arm. We joined the bustle of people, many of whom admired Zephyr and asking how I'd made him.

Although I gave vague comments about acquiring him the way he was, people still shot him envious looks. Clearly, if I entered any cosplay competition, I'd win with such a lifelike dragon by my side, but I didn't plan on drawing any more attention to myself.

After several painstaking minutes while I tried to act normal and Minsheng and Daisy kept a lookout, the other cosplayers slowly formed into a group to parade out.

I made sure we were near the middle, but I still didn't know how we'd get out of the store without the two on the doors seeing us. We needed to distract them as we went past. But how?

As we got closer to the doors, I saw the perfect opportunity. The agents had been engaged by some other cosplayers who clearly thought the agents had dressed up as the characters from a film. The cosplayers were trying to strike up a conversation on the subject. Drawing in a burst of air, I waited for the moment we were most likely to be spotted and jetted it at the back of the female cosplayer.

It knocked her off her feet into the arms of the first agent with so much force he wobbled and bumped into the second agent. Finally, we had a clear window.

Looking away and trying to go faster, I hurried out of the store with the parade, making sure Zephyr and the others were with me.

CHAPTER EIGHT

"Oh my, that was close," Daisy whispered a few minutes later when we were heading through the mall. I joined the other cosplayers in waving at onlookers.

It felt surreal. If I hadn't been worrying about a secret government organization making me and Zephyr disappear at any moment, it would have been fun—a great way to take Zephyr out in public and not make the world panic.

While we'd been changing our clothes, the agents had restored order, and a few people who had seen us come through the first time now spotted Zephyr again. The looks of relief when they assumed he was an elaborate cosplay accessory were comical. Part of me wanted to step out of the crowd and show he was real. What good did it do to hide his true nature?

Instead, I stayed where I was, spotting more agents by the open doors of the mall. Most of the agents were doing as I'd have expected, calming people and rescuing their own fallen. Some were heading back to their SUVs and leaving, but it was clear they knew we were in the mall and were trying to make sure we didn't get out.

"So what now?" I asked as Minsheng and Chris came closer again, all of us huddling in the cosplay crowd to try to avoid detection. The parade had spread out a little, making it impossible to get past the next set of agents the same way we had the first. We needed to do something else.

"Do you think Newton can trigger the fire detectors?" Minsheng asked.

I'll ask him, Zephyr sent into my head.

Make it quick.

There was a pause as I waited, Zephyr making low noises near Newton.

He said he probably can, but he doesn't know what one is or where he'd find it.

"Yes, if one of us can get him to a good spot."

"I will," Daisy volunteered without missing a beat. "I've always wanted to cuddle a fire salamander."

I gently handed him over, the little guy still wrapped up in my cardigan and mostly out of sight. My worries over what would happen to the cardigan came a fraction too late to warn Daisy as she hurried to one side of the mall and near the entrance of a shop with Newton.

Every second after dragged like it was a thousand. The parade continued to press forward, giving us little choice but to move with it, and each step took us closer to danger and being spotted.

"Come on, Daisy," I said under my breath. "What's taking so long?"

I think they've noticed me, Zephyr said.

Shitsticks.

I was just about to get Minsheng and Chris' attention to make a run for it when the fire alarm began to wail and all the sprinklers switched on.

Chaos ensued.

Go with the crowds and keep low, I told Zephyr.

Not sure I could do anything else.

As the shops all started to empty of people, the crowds around us grew. With everyone shouting and yelling and screaming, we were rushed along with the tide of cosplayers and shoppers as they tried to hurry outside.

The agents had no choice but to get out of the way as more and more people flooded out. Keeping low and among the cosplayers as they formed a huddle, we got out the front door.

"We need to find Daisy," Minsheng said, trying to look around, but people were still rushing out of the mall, and we still had little choice but to follow.

More than a little tense and wary of how Zephyr was getting crushed in the crowd, I tried to push forward. We'd made it past the nearest black sedans when an agent spotted us. He reached into the open door of the nearest car like he was going to grab a radio.

Not sure what else to do, I sent a burst of air to slam the door into him. It knocked him off-balance and gave Zephyr a chance to leap forward and exhale gas at the vulnerable man. He inhaled it before he knew what was happening. A moment later, he slumped over the driver's seat.

"Did your dragon just attack another cosplayer?" someone asked, staring at us like we'd just grown three heads. I didn't know how to answer, my mind freezing. Chris patted the guy dressed as some kind of anime character on the shoulder.

"Do you believe in dragons?" he asked.

The anime kid slowly shook his head, but he hesitated like he was doubting what would have previously been a very solid conviction. I fought back a smile as Daisy hurried through the crowd from the side, spotting us. She wasn't carrying my cardigan anymore, and Newton was resting on her shoulder, making her cosplay outfit look even more epic.

"Right, time to get out of here," I said, charging across the street. We pushed out of the cosplay crowd and away from all the agents and people. A couple of times I glanced back, but if any agents were nearby, they were too busy stopping the crowds from vandalizing their cars by mistake, and people were still trying to get out of the mall and into the surrounding area.

I shook my head as we hurried around the next corner and into a nearby park. Although we were dressed in cosplay outfits, so Zephyr could be considered a prop, we were still getting people pointing at us, cars were honking their horns, and far too much attention. When I saw someone snapping photos of Zephyr and us, I knew we couldn't carry on like this.

"We need to get Zephyr out of the public's view and into something like a van," I said. "And fast."

"What do you propose? We don't have anywhere to go. Or a car anymore," Minsheng shot back.

Frowning at the antagonistic response, I dived down

the next alley I saw. Thankfully, they all followed, but I knew we wouldn't have long.

"We either need to find a building we can lie low in or another van. Anyone got any ideas about how we could acquire either?" I asked. My apartment was gone now, the lease up, and we were in a part of LA I didn't know very well, so I couldn't help solve the problem.

"What if I hire us a van?" Daisy said a moment later. "And we rent a motel room and sneak Zephyr in the back way?"

"That's better than what I was thinking," Minsheng replied.

I raised my eyebrows, wanting to ask what that had been, but a cop siren nearby reminded us we didn't have a lot of time. Now wasn't a good time to stop and have an argument.

"Where's the nearest place we can rent a van?" I asked. For a moment, no one said anything. Rolling my eyes, I pulled the cheap new phone I'd bought out of my bag and did a quick internet search.

There was one about a mile away, but there was no way to be sure they had a van. I showed it to Daisy anyway.

"We can't stay here with Zephyr while Daisy gets a van," Chris said. "We've got to move out before the agents come this way. You said they tracked you before, right? And were monitoring social media?"

I nodded. They'd pulled my first photo of Zephyr's egg off my social media and my phone and then come to take the egg. That was what had started all this.

For a moment, I felt trapped. I hadn't asked for this. I hadn't asked for any of it.

I can fly, Zephyr's voice said in my head. *Why don't I just fly off and find somewhere safe where they can't reach me?*

No, I replied. *You're not going anywhere without me, and besides, they want me as much as you now.*

Zephyr's words did give me an idea, though. Why couldn't we all go up?

Looking at the building beside us, I noticed an outside fire escape. Although the ladder was up, I walked over to it.

Can you fly up there and unhook the ladder? I asked the dragon.

He looked up and tilted his head to the side. A moment later, he jumped and flapped his wings, almost catching them on the walls on either side. If he'd been much bigger, he'd never have been able to get in the air in such a small space.

Landing on the bottom platform with a slight clatter, Zephyr folded his wings up again. He barely fit, but he moved toward the ladder and managed to unhook it with his mouth.

Not explaining to the others, I began to climb. Thankfully, they either understood or were willing to follow me in whatever I had planned because Minsheng and Chris climbed after me.

Meet you at the top. Zephyr leaped from the platform, flapping again and pulling himself up the side of the building until he reached the top and disappeared over the ledge.

Sighing and once more annoyed at myself that I couldn't yet fly, I made my way up the ladders. Chris came last and pulled up the bottom ladder behind him. Hopefully it would make it harder for the agents to work out where we'd gone.

The evening sun was bright on my face when we reached the roof. For a moment I basked in it, noticing Zephyr was doing the same.

We were on top of a relatively large building not far from the center of LA. In the distance towered the taller skyscrapers, but they were far enough away I wasn't worried about us being seen. A few closer buildings were a little taller, but there was a nice shady spot behind the stairwell that would hide us from the view of anyone in them.

Hoping we wouldn't be there long, I sat in the shade to wait. Immediately, Newton tried to get down. I placed him on the floor, noticing his foot was much better and he was bearing some of his weight on his broken limb.

The fire salamander moved to a patch of sunshine not far away and stayed there. I could only assume he was basking in the heat of the evening sun. Was this what his family had been doing the night before when the agents and other people had tried to capture them?

I felt so angry I would have attacked any agent on sight. Was it really so hard not to feel threatened and leave creatures like Newton and even Zephyr alone?

I knew the answer. Humanity was scared of anything that was different, especially if it was possibly powerful. The human race was so insecure about its own position in the world and so selfish about its own needs that it couldn't be kind, it couldn't share, and it couldn't trust.

I knew I had to make a stand, and the last couple of hours had shown me that I also somehow needed to show people that all the creatures and races they thought were myths lived among them and meant no harm.

But first, I was going to have to send the agency a message—another one. We weren't going to quietly disappear, and we weren't going to stop living normal lives.

I was still thinking about the best way to get the agency to leave us alone when Minsheng got a message from Daisy to let us know she'd managed to hire a van. We just had a few more minutes to wait.

While we were waiting, I heard a car pull up on the street below, and several people got out. Although I couldn't hear what they were saying, it was clear multiple individuals were talking as they came down the alley we'd been in moments before.

I moved closer to the edge so I could listen.

"If they were here," someone said, "they're not now."

"People don't just disappear into thin air," another replied.

"These aren't normal people. How do we know they don't just disappear into thin air?"

"Because if they could do that, they'd have done it when we attacked them and not run through a mall first."

This shut the first speaker up, and the footsteps receded. Eventually, they got back in the car and drove off.

Not long after, the rest of my companions came closer, all of us more than ready to go back down the ladder and get off this roof. Daisy should have been here by now.

I was just about to suggest we go down anyway when Minsheng got another message.

"Daisy says someone is watching the alley, so she

doesn't want to pull up and make it obvious she is picking us up."

I nodded, glad she'd noticed and decided to be so cautious. It left us only one way out, however—down the stairs in the middle of the building.

Hurrying over to the access, I found out it was locked.

Before I could ask if any of them knew how to get in, Chris pulled a set of lock picks out of his pocket and began jiggering the lock.

It took him a moment, but eventually, he had the door open.

"You're going to have to teach me how to do that," I said.

"As soon as we're somewhere safe, you're on." Chris was the first to go into the building, leading us downstairs.

Zephyr and I went last, Newton cradled in my arms again. After his stint in the sun, he was even warmer than he had been before. If he'd been any other animal, I'd have been worried about him.

The stairwell ran down the center of the staff area of a hotel. A couple of times, Chris motioned for us to go through a door to hide or head back up a flight of stairs so a member of staff could pass without noticing us.

With the alley being watched, I knew we couldn't go out through the front of the hotel, which meant we had to find a way out the back. And the lower we went in the building, the busier it got.

"I think we're going to have to act like cosplayers again," I said when we'd been stuck on the third floor for several minutes.

"That's not going to be as easy when there's just three of us," Minsheng replied.

"We could just pretend we're staying at the hotel. As long as we're talking loudly about some kind of cosplay, I'm sure people will buy it. They don't want to believe in dragons. People would rather think he's a really, really good prop."

Minsheng sighed, but eventually, he nodded.

"This had better work," I heard him mutter. Choosing to ignore it, I placed a hand on Zephyr's shoulder and guided us down the hall past the hotel rooms.

"Hurry, guys, or we're going to miss the best costume awards," I said when I saw the first set of people. At the same time, I sped up a little.

Although the passersby gave us looks, this seemed to satisfy them.

I applied the same tactic when we saw more people. By the time we were down to the bottom floor, all of us were having a conversation about an imaginary cosplay convention.

Once we were on the bottom floor, I put my back to the main entrance and headed the other way. We passed a pool and a dining room and kept going. As soon as I saw a fire exit on the back of the building, I pushed it open and walked out.

We came out in another alley, this one wide enough for delivery vehicles and clearly where the hotel brought in supplies.

Minsheng started tapping on his phone. Within seconds, he'd summoned Daisy to us. She pulled up in a plain black van and got the back doors open.

I had Zephyr climb in first and followed him. This time Minsheng rode in the passenger seat while Chris got in the back with us.

After the doors closed and Daisy pulled away, I exhaled, feeling most of the tension leave my body. For a little while at least, we were safe again.

CHAPTER NINE

Daisy drove us the rest of the way to the beach. Once there, she pulled into the parking lot and shut off the engine.

"We should wait until dark," I said. "Then we should look for Newton's family."

"I'll get us some dinner," Daisy replied.

"You'll need an extra pair of hands." Chris slipped out the back. "And my bladder isn't what it used to be."

"I should find a quiet spot and contact the organization," Minsheng said before sighing. "They might have some options for us."

At first I thought about protesting that Zephyr, Newton, and I were being left in the van by ourselves, but I wanted a chance to listen in on the agency and see if I could figure out what their next move would be. Watching Minsheng go, I made myself comfortable, Zephyr curled up against me on one side and Newton on my lap.

I pulled the transceiver out of my bag and switched it on. There was a small amount of recorded chatter from early that morning, no doubt what would have been the command to take Zephyr and me. I'd listen to that bit if I had time.

Only half an hour ago, it had begun recording again. I hit play on that section of audio.

"I take it from your face that you still don't have her or the dragon," the familiar voice of the woman in charge of the agency said.

"It's just a matter of time. She can't elude me forever, not even in LA. The dragon alone will draw plenty of attention," the voice of Mr. In Charge replied.

I smiled, knowing he was going to have to try a lot harder, especially after he'd been stunned by one of his own darts earlier in the day.

"You promised you would have her back here in time for lunch. It's now dinner time, and I don't see her."

"Given you weren't even trying to catch her and that beast until the agency sent me to find out why a dragon who was supposed to be dead was seen aiding even more creatures in escaping from your agents, you aren't in the position to make demands."

I lifted an eyebrow. Clearly, the buck didn't stop with Agent Crawley, nor with the new man in charge, but that might have to be yet another problem for me to sort out another day.

"As I said before, she was staying hidden and posing me no problems at all."

"Of course," Mr. In Charge replied, disdain clear in his voice. "Your little promise to leave each other alone. She broke it in, what, about eight weeks?"

"It was a mutually beneficial arrangement. She kept the dragon out of sight and only took it to the beach now and then in the middle of the night, and I didn't have to keep cleaning up mess after mess or explaining why she had trashed yet another location. But you can guarantee that won't be the case going forward."

"It was never going to be the case going forward. She has a dragon. Do you know how big they get? By next year, it will be the size of your office, and she'll be flying around on its back. Another year after that, her dragon will be the size of a small house."

This tirade was met with silence.

"But let me guess, you thought by then she wouldn't be your problem. She'd have taken her dragon somewhere safer, or you'd have been promoted. Sitting behind a desk in a more controlled environment."

"She wasn't a problem. Of course the dragon would have grown. But we're not going to know if she'd have taken the dragon to the Rockies along with all the others, would we? You've come here and forced her hand."

"No, your incompetence is the reason I'm here. The people higher up felt you needed a hand from someone with experience in catching dragons."

I was stunned. There were more dragons? Zephyr wasn't the only one? The fact that Mr. In Charge had caught others only made me feel even angrier.

You hear that, Zephyr? There might be more like you. Possibly more like us.

Not if these people have their way.

They're not going to. We'll find a way to stop them.

My eyes met Zephyr's, the same shade of violet, my words a promise.

"Why are you here, Knox? Why let them send you to my

city? You're clearly out of your depth here. You wouldn't be in my office if you had any leads."

"We know where they are," Knox replied. "I have my agents watching the hotel they've hidden in right now. They were seen inside, pretending to be cosplayers. Fooled the staff, but they won't fool us."

"Then you'd better get back there and bring them in, shouldn't you? I hope you haven't forgotten that you answer to me while you're here, even if your presence wasn't requested."

This ended the conversation, the sound of a door slamming shortly after. I exhaled as I switched it off, nothing more on the feed. At least they didn't know we'd left the hotel. It gave us a respite. I could just imagine the trouble Agent Knox was going to get into when Ms. Crawley was informed that Zephyr and I were no longer at the hotel.

Relieved, I stroked my dragon's scales and contemplated our future. Could there really be more dragons and elves out there?

Daisy and Chris came back, the takeout bags in their hands full to the brim. Zephyr sniffed as they opened the doors, clearly hungry, and Newton seemed interested.

There was more food than I'd expected, but as Zephyr chowed down some of the meatier dishes, I realized it wouldn't go far enough and set some aside for Minsheng.

While we ate, I let them know the good news I'd listened to. It was a relief to everyone to know we weren't being hunted right now.

"The rest of the family are all okay too. No one turned up at Minsheng's other businesses," Daisy replied.

"Probably because they think they know where we are,"

Chris said as he put his empty container down. "Once they realize we're not there, they're bound to look for other possibilities."

I gulped, feeling guilty, but I wasn't sure what I could do. For the first time, I considered giving ourselves up so they wouldn't bother Minsheng and his family any longer.

"They won't hurt them, will they?" I asked.

"No. One of the reasons Minsheng has them at the restaurants he does is because there would be too many witnesses, no matter what time of night or day it is."

I nodded, reassured for now, but I would have to consider the safety of my friends carefully in the future.

By the time we had all finished eating, I was getting worried about Minsheng. He'd been gone for an hour, and I imagined the agents noticing him and trying to take him in. I didn't put it above this Knox to capture my mentor and friend to try to get me to turn up and save him. It was the kind of situation he knew I'd respond to.

Thankfully, before I could voice my concern out loud, Minsheng came back, hurrying across the parking lot before getting into the back of the van. I sighed, more than a little relieved, but he had a very serious look on his face and didn't start on his food right away.

"What did they say?" I asked, not sure I wanted to know but not happy the suspense.

"They're saddened that we couldn't continue our truce with the agency. They said it had given them hope that as long as mythicals were careful, they might one day live in this world peacefully. Obviously, not everyone in the agency feels as if we should be left in peace."

"And?" I asked, feeling like Minsheng was skirting another topic.

"They think we should leave LA immediately. In fact, I've been ordered to leave. Given the address of a safe house we can go to nearby. They've told me we'll get further instructions there."

"No," I replied. "I'm not giving up. Not after what I've heard."

Minsheng opened his mouth, but I cut him off and told him about the conversation I'd just heard, aware Daisy and Chris were listening in. It had to be had said, though. I couldn't leave now. I just couldn't. Not only did I think Agent Knox would simply follow us, but I'd beaten them once, and I was sure I could do it again.

"As much as I can see your point, Aella, I don't think you understand. I work for the organization. They pay for everything, and they've commanded me to leave."

"So leave," I replied, folding my arms across my chest. I knew I was being a brat and coming across as stubborn, but I couldn't help it. I wasn't running away, especially when others needed our help.

"I can't leave without you. I'm sworn to protect you. You're my ward, and the organization will hold me accountable for your actions."

"Perfect," I replied. "You can tell them I won't leave, so you've got to stay to protect me."

In the front of the van, Daisy snorted. Minsheng shot her a withering look, but she just shrugged.

"I think they want us to go find the Sanctuary," Minsheng said. "We'd be safe there, among others of our kind."

"I thought the Sanctuary was a myth!" Chris exclaimed, sitting up as if this were the most fascinating thing any of us had said.

"No. The organization has interacted with it before. It's as real as you and me."

"And you're only telling us this now?" Chris asked. "How come I didn't know about it? I'm part of the organization too."

"You are?" I asked, glancing at Chris.

"Of course. Why else do you think I turn up with tech and gadgets and help you out all the time? I mean, don't get me wrong; it's fun and all that. But if they catch me, I'm a goner. I could be living a quiet life as a hardware engineer. The organization pays me well to make you gear and help out. But I still don't get why I didn't know about the Sanctuary. I'm part gnome. I belong there."

"It's a closely guarded secret. I've only known it was real for a year or so and only had the authority to tell all of you for the last ten minutes."

"As awesome as the Sanctuary sounds, we can't just run away. The agency is going to hunt me down no matter where I go."

"The Sanctuary is very good at hiding," Minsheng said. "And you can grow stronger there."

It's worth considering, Zephyr said in my head. I glared at him.

You want to run away as well?

No. I'd very much like to eat this Agent Knox and the woman he answers to, but the Sanctuary is a place in my memories, and I think we would like it there.

I smiled at the thought of Zephyr eating Miss Cool, but I knew we were a long way from that being a reality.

"I get what the organization is trying to do. I do. They want to keep me safe."

"They want you to live long enough to train hard—"

"And one day win this fight," I finished, cutting Minsheng off.

He nodded, confirming what I'd suspected.

"Then they might need to trust me. This woman in charge only wants us to be out of her hair for a while. She doesn't care if Zephyr and I are still around. Not right now. She wants Agent Knox gone, and she wants to get back to her normal job."

"So, what? You think you can get her to agree to ignore us again?" Minsheng demanded.

"It's worth a try. Take Knox out of the picture and then ask her again. We just need a place to go that's big enough for Zephyr as he grows. The organization was working on it. What if I could find somewhere?"

You know how big I'm going to get, right?

Yes. I heard them. As big as a small house. But LA is full of warehouses far bigger than that.

We don't own any warehouses.

No, but I know where an abandoned one is.

Zephyr stared at me. I pictured the building I'd found him in, wondering if he could see what was in my memories.

That might work, but the others would need to agree. We can't force anyone to stay with us.

Wouldn't dream of it. You snore.

Zephyr let out a low snort, then grinned. It helped ease

the tension I felt as I explained the conversation Zephyr and I had just had.

"Will the organization agree to us hiding somewhere that's actually big enough?" I asked once I'd finished.

"They might, but I make no promises."

"Okay," I replied, taking what I could get. "In the meantime, I think we should help Newton get back to his family. Rescuing him started all this. It would be wrong to abandon him now."

This melted Minsheng's resolve. One glance at the fire salamander and he sighed.

"All right. We help Newton get home, then I'll come with you to check out this warehouse. But if we have any trouble on the way, or we can't easily get Knox to give up, we go find the Sanctuary. Deal?"

"Deal," I replied, knowing I wouldn't give up until Knox wasn't a problem anymore. Minsheng might have gotten used to hiding, but I was used to going about my life like an ordinary citizen. If I was truly the descendant of a great dragonrider, I wasn't going to hide and pretend I wasn't.

I didn't deny that the Sanctuary sounded like somewhere I would want to visit one day. But I didn't want to be forced to go there. If I went to the Sanctuary, it would be on my terms.

CHAPTER TEN

While we waited for the sun to set and the world to get darker, we sat in the back of the van and played cards. It turned out Chris carried a pack with him wherever he went.

"I still can't believe you didn't tell me the Sanctuary actually existed," Chris said. We'd been playing for a little while, and the conversation had lulled while Minsheng dealt another hand.

"The only way it survives is by the people knowing about it being very secretive," Minsheng said as he put down another card.

"Yeah, I can understand that. But I've been helping you for years."

"I don't know where it is. No one in the organization seems to know that, just that it's real, and it's here in America. Didn't seem like it was worth telling anyone."

"What is the Sanctuary?" I asked, taking the chance to pose my questions. "Is it a place?"

"I think it's more nomadic than that. They travel. It

stops people from getting too suspicious if they don't stay in the same place for long.

"It also makes them harder to find, I bet," Chris added.

Minsheng nodded but didn't say any more.

"Are there others like me in the Sanctuary?" I asked a few minutes later.

"I don't think so, but I don't know for sure. Most of the elves are gone, and the creatures they bond with too. That's why being your Shishou is such an honor."

I blushed, not sure how I felt about being considered special. I mean, don't get me wrong, everyone wants to be special. But the fate-of-the-world-on-my-shoulders kind of special came with a whole lot of pressure.

It did make me even more determined to sort out this agency problem before I went in search of the Sanctuary, however. I didn't want to turn up on their doorstep being thought of as some kind of savior and bringing danger I couldn't handle with me.

"It's pretty dark now," Daisy said, the only one still sitting in the front, reading a book. "And I haven't seen anyone for a while. We could probably look for Newton's family now."

I put down my hand of cards, not even finishing the round. I'd had enough of being inside the cramped van. Going to find Newton's family would be a much-needed break.

Minsheng grabbed the temperature detection device and switched it on as Chris moved to the front of the van and put the key in the ignition.

"I'll drive around, and you let me know when we're

getting warmer," Chris said with a grin, clearly amused by his own pun.

I rolled my eyes but looked away as I did it so I could also smile. These guys might not have been the kind of people I'd have chosen for friends before all of this had happened but I was really beginning to like them.

As Chris drove and Minsheng tried to direct him, I soon sighed. Although the view was changing, different kinds of houses and areas of the beach front going by, it still involved an awful lot of me just sitting in the back of the van not doing much. It turned out the different activity wasn't that different after all.

I tried to focus on Newton, checking he was okay and giving him some extra water. Already the little guy's leg was pretty much okay, and I slowly unwrapped the splint and bandages so he could walk more easily.

"A lot of the mythicals heal faster than humans. Pretty much the only way they survive," Daisy said when she noticed my surprise.

As if Newton had understood my words, he darted around the inside of the van, running at a speed I wouldn't have thought possible had I not seen him coming close to it on the beach while injured the night before. It was still a marvel to behold, especially up close.

It made me wonder how many other mythicals were hiding amongst the population of Earth. They were clearly good at evading capture and the notice of other people.

When we were still driving around an hour later and no closer to finding Newton's family, I'd had enough. I'd been in the back of the van for at least eight hours, and it was all too much. Given the way Zephyr shuffled around and occasionally tried to wriggle his wings, I didn't think I was the only one.

"This isn't working, and I can't stand being in here any longer," I said. "Pull over somewhere, Chris. We'll try to find Newton's family a different way."

"The agency will have everyone looking for you," Minsheng pointed out.

"I know, but it's the middle of the night. And I can't stay in a van for the rest of my life. Zephyr and Newton can communicate. Perhaps they can help us find Newton's family and everyone can stretch their legs a bit.

"I'm willing to give it a try," Chris said. "It's not like we're getting anywhere with this method. I guess my device isn't sensitive enough."

Minsheng frowned and for a moment didn't reply. I could tell he was thinking and I didn't interrupt. No doubt he was concerned for me, and I appreciated it, but he couldn't shield me from everything.

"All right. We'll look for Newton's family a different way. Daisy and Chris can try to find the family on foot with his device and you and me and Zephyr can try to use Zephyr to find them."

That all right with you? I asked Zephyr, almost grateful he could read my thoughts.

I need to get out of this van.

You and me both, buddy. You and me both.

I'm also hungry.

When are you not hungry?

He gave me a look. I smiled but patted him on the back.

I'm sure we can find a moment to get you some more food. Is there anything in particular you'd like?

That pizza we had the last time we were up to nighttime antics was amazing.

I'm not sure dragons should be allowed to eat pizza.

We can eat a lot more than you humans think we can.

I tilted my head to the side, studying him. Was I getting my dragon addicted to junk food?

I didn't get any more time to think about it, or ask Zephyr or even Minsheng if there was a special diet that dragons were supposed to eat. Chris pulled over by the side of a road out of the way and drew our attention back to our task.

Only waiting a moment to check if the coast was clear, I pushed open the back door and got out. I almost fell over, my legs feeling strange from the lack of use.

Zephyr wasn't much better, sort of tumbling out of the back of the van, but as soon as he was clear he outstretched both wings, his head tilted up and his eyes closed, a delighted smile on his face. I stretched as well, pretty sure I didn't feel as good as Zephyr did right now.

The others all followed, Daisy locking the car.

"We'll let you know if we find Newton's family. If you find them first, meet back here when you're done." Daisy took the device from Minsheng and walked away before either of us could reply. Chris hurried after her, glancing over his shoulder at us with an almost reluctant sort of look.

"Come on then," Minsheng said. "I don't want to be out in the open any longer than we have to."

Okay, Zephyr, I said. *Where does Newton think we should start?*

For a moment Zephyr didn't reply, the only sound the little roars and grunts the two of them exchanged.

He thinks they'll be down by the beach not far from where they were separated. They have a designated meeting spot where everyone tries to get to if something goes wrong.

And you're only telling us this now?

We only asked him now. And I'm not sure he'd have trusted us if we'd asked him much sooner. His kind don't trust humans. And despite all of you having some kind of different heritage, to a fire salamander you all look human.

Good point.

As Zephyr and Newton started walking down the road, I followed.

"They said we should go this way," I told Minsheng, leaving out the rest.

For a few minutes we walked along parallel to the beach, heading down quiet roads full of houses. At this time of night almost everyone was fast asleep.

"You know, this isn't exactly being discreet," Minsheng said as he caught up. "We've got a dragon and a fire salamander walking down the street in front of us."

"No one's awake," I replied, but I was reassuring myself as much as him. The last thing we wanted to do was attract more attention.

I thought for a moment as we wandered along. Maybe we could do this a little safer.

Zephyr, I thought, trying to get the dragon's attention.

Why don't you fly for a bit? You might even be able to see his family better from up there.

You're worried about me, aren't you?

I'm pretty sure I'm allowed to worry about you.

You are. I'll fly. It's not like I really need the excuse. I'm beginning to get more memories of what it feels like to fly in complete freedom. Maybe one day we can both do the same.

I couldn't reply, a lump in my throat. I'd been so concerned with how trapped I felt I hadn't thought about what Zephyr would feel like.

As Zephyr launched into the air I sighed. It always felt slightly wrong when he flew away from me and left me behind on the ground.

"You'll be able to follow him soon. I'm sure," Minsheng said as I looked up. A moment later my mentor scooped up the fire salamander and placed it on his shoulder.

I could only hope he was right. Being stuck on the ground while the creature I felt part of flew in the air above me felt so wrong I was never entirely comfortable on the ground anymore.

I think I see the place Newton described, Zephyr's voice boomed in my head. I winced at the loudness. *Keep going straight and take the second right. There's...*

Zephyr didn't finish the sentence and instantly I looked up, fear flourishing inside me in seconds. Was he okay?

There's what? I asked instead, trying to sound as calm as I could.

Agents.

I stopped, almost freezing to the spot. Minsheng only needed to take one look at my face to know there was trouble ahead.

"Where?" he asked. I repeated the question as a thought and could only hope that Zephyr could hear me. He seemed to be flying farther away.

Behind you. That's why I didn't notice them at first. They look like they're doing some kind of sweeping patrol. Coming your way.

Instantly I started walking again and looked back over my shoulder. I could just about see the outline of several butch men as they walked this way.

Minsheng picked up the pace along with me, and we hurried toward the next junction before taking a right toward the beach. The sound of waves crashing on sand came to my ears, followed by the smell of salt water and the feel of a soft breeze on my face. If I hadn't been on the run from agents again, I'd have enjoyed a moment to stop and appreciate it.

How many of them are there? I asked Zephyr once they were momentarily out of sight.

Lots. They all pulled up not far from the van. I think someone must have seen us. They started searching there and then came this way.

"We need to get back to the van, and get you all safe," Minsheng said, his words overlapping with Zephyr's.

"There's no safe route back. Not at the moment," I replied as I jogged onward.

Can you keep an eye on them and direct us to safety without being spotted? I asked Zephyr, ignoring Minsheng as he protested and tried to stop me.

I think so, but only while this cloud holds.

It's more important that they don't see you than that we get information.

You can't outrun them forever.

No, but we can lead them away from the van and then Chris and Daisy can get back to it, at least.

I'll do my best. Zephyr seemed to fly farther away, and I had the vague feeling that he'd also dropped behind, no doubt to see what Chris and Daisy faced.

"Let Chris and Daisy know there's agents and we're aborting, but make them wait a few minutes. If they head back to the van too soon, they'll just bump into the back of the squad of agents. And we need to keep the van a secret."

"I'm less concerned about the van than you and Zephyr," Minsheng replied as he pulled out his phone.

"We won't be able to get another vehicle easily. If the agents work out that the van is ours, that's it. We can't make a car chase work in our favor. Not until both Zephyr and I can fly and attack cars."

Minsheng sighed, but nodded and began tapping out a message. Hopefully he'd convey everything needed but be brief. Who knew if anyone was monitoring the communications? These were new phones only used to message each other, but the agency had done surprising things already to perfectly normal technology.

I could attack a car now, Zephyr's voice sounded in my head, making it clear he'd heard our conversation.

Maybe, but there are lots of agents, and I'd have to hide in a car. I don't want you to be in all that danger alone.

Me neither.

As we turned left onto the beach, I noticed some agents were already farther down and coming this way. Sticking close to the shadows by the houses, we crept along at the fastest pace we dared.

Newton's family is just up on the left, Zephyr said. *But the agents are moving quickly.*

I growled, frustrated and not sure how we were going to get out of this again. It was as if the agents were permanently just one step ahead of us.

CHAPTER ELEVEN

"Daisy and Chris can see the van, and the agents are leaving it behind," Minsheng said as he finished reading a message. "Looks like they're trying to form some kind of net around us."

"Oh, great," I replied, already fed up with trying to creep along with agents behind us. More of them coming from in front would really piss me off.

Are you seeing the same thing? I asked Zephyr a moment later, pausing by the edge of a building so I could check the next road was clear.

It appears so. More agents are now coming toward you from the other end of the beach.

Crapsicles.

I didn't move, caught in indecision. Could we maybe fight our way out? Zephyr had made it sound like there could be even more than at the restaurant earlier in the day, and I didn't think I could do that level of magic again. Not yet.

"We need to find a way out of it," Minsheng said as he spotted the very thing Zephyr had just informed us of.

"Zephyr can fly over, so it's just you and me," I said as I realized we were being circled, more agents now coming down the side street.

"Suggestions?"

I looked around, although I was pretty sure my mentor was supposed to be suggesting ways we could solve problems, not me. Either way, we needed somewhere to either hide, or a way to move past the agents without them detecting us.

"Can you swim? I asked, looking at the ocean.

"Well enough? Can you?" He glanced left and right as if he was going to run to the beach anyway.

I thought about the last time I'd swum. I'd barely ever tried to swim in the sea, always preferring swimming pools. But I could swim. You didn't live near a beach like the ones in LA and not learn how to swim. It's just that I knew there was a significant difference between swimming along the shore, and swimming far enough out that people on the shore couldn't see you. The dark would help, but the water would be cold enough that we were going to want towels on the other end at the very least.

With no better ideas coming to mind and the agents closing in, I knew we had no option. I ran for the water's edge along with Minsheng and hoped I could swim well enough.

"What about our clothes?" I asked Minsheng as I stopped at the edge and crouched low to pull off my shoes and socks, trying to ignore the tension in my shoulders and my racing heart. I needed to keep calm and keep thinking straight.

"Bundle everything into your top," he said, not so much as glancing my way. "Then balance it on your head with one hand if you can. I've seen people do it before."

I gulped at the thought of doing that as well as trying to swim, but I guessed I was about to find out how easy it truly was. Hesitating for just a moment, I quickly pulled my pants off, rolled them up and then yanked my t-shirt off too. Feeling more than a little exposed, I waded forward as I wrapped everything in my t-shirt. It was barely big enough, but I soon had it bunched up, my hand holding the bundle shut.

Until I was farther out, I didn't stuff it on my head, but Minsheng was already ahead of me and wading out. Thankfully the waves were calm enough that they were breaking at waist height. I quickly moved through and then caught up with Minsheng. As the water grew closer to Newton he began to get more agitated, until Minsheng had to move him to his bundle.

"The people I watched doing this made it look a lot easier," Minsheng whispered as he tried to balance his own bundle and Newton on his head and almost went under.

"I doubt they were trying to get away from an army of government agents hell-bent on their destruction," I whispered back, getting deep enough I had to decide what to do with my own bundle. For now I merely held it up, but it wasn't easy to swim with one arm in the air.

I heard Minsheng chuckle as we both continued to get deeper. The tide was on its way out for now, but it had been pretty low so I felt fairly confident it would turn and head back in soon, and take us back to shore before we could get into too much trouble. I couldn't decide if that was a comforting fact, because of the threat awaiting us on the beach, but it was in my head already.

And no sooner had I thought about the tide than I imagined getting swept out to sea and needing to make a fuss and attract attention from the very people we were trying to hide from. And I clearly wasn't the only one bothered by being in the water this far from land. Newton kept letting out little noises, and he appeared to be shivering on the very top of Minsheng's bundle.

"I think Newton is scared," I added as I turned and looked at the shore for a moment. I moved my free arm and my legs in gentle motions to keep afloat, grateful the night was calm enough we weren't being battered by strong waves, although we bobbed up and down on the swell.

With the agents on the other side of the waves, we couldn't easily hear them, but they didn't appear to be looking our way and they weren't very far off from meeting in the middle.

"Best thing we can do for all of us is get somewhere safer. We should probably swim in parallel to the beach for now," Minsheng said as he also turned. "We don't want to be in their direct line of sight when they realize we're not in their net anymore."

I didn't answer as Minsheng continued swimming, merely concentrating on doing the same. Although I was fairly fit and I was faring okay so far, I still worried that this task would prove to be beyond my abilities. The sooner we were far enough down the coast and back on dry land the better.

The next few minutes were almost peaceful. It still felt odd to be carrying my footwear and clothing on my head, but I'd begun getting into a rhythm and the agents slowly fell behind us. Maybe we could do this after all.

But the farther we went, the more my limbs tired, and I noticed with increasing fear that we were getting farther and farther from the shoreline. The beach and the agents grew smaller and the night more quiet.

"I think we should probably head for shore now," I said when I couldn't stay quiet any longer, but no sooner had I uttered the words than there were shouts from somewhere behind. We both looked back, but the agents didn't seem to be yelling at us. Instead they were having an argument, two very clearly in each other's faces.

"Wonder what that's about?" Minsheng whispered.

I didn't know, and I wasn't sure I dared answer. It was almost too much to hope that we'd slip through their net because of their internal strife. We'd be lucky if that was the result.

Swimming for a little longer, I noticed the noises had died down, and another glance over my shoulder showed the agents slowly combing the area they'd reached before they fanned back out. My limbs almost gave out right then and there. If they came back up the beach before heading back to their vehicles we'd have to swim for even longer.

Daisy and Chris have moved the van, Zephyr said, reminding me he was still out there, watching. If I was tired from all the swimming, I didn't doubt all the flying would be wearing him out as well.

Let us know if the agents suspect we're in the water.

They don't at the moment. One of them thinks I flew you all to safety.

Is that what the argument was about?

No, that was about who was in charge. It seems the agents we fought before don't like the new ones.

I don't either. My thoughts trailed off as the ache in my limbs got to the point I could barely think of anything else.

"I need to head to shore," I said aloud, already panicked I'd left it too late.

Minsheng didn't reply, but he turned toward the shore and began swimming in that direction instead.

For now the tide was still going out, and it felt like no matter how hard we swam for the shore it was still just as far away.

Exhausted, I had to stop swimming for a moment and just tread water. Fear filled me. Was I in way over my head?

"I don't know if I can do this," I said when Minsheng noticed I wasn't following him and stopped as well.

"Me neither, but that's often the way. I didn't know if I could mentor you when we first met. I still don't know for sure I can keep you safe. But I'm not going to give up. Because if we stop trying, we definitely won't succeed."

I nodded, not sure I had the strength to say anything more and aware he'd probably just expended an awful lot of energy to give me a pep talk. Gratitude and warmth toward Minsheng flooded through me, and with it the desire to fight on. If for no other reason than I wanted to show him that he wasn't failing.

I tried to focus just on Minsheng a little way ahead of me, and putting my arm out again and again and kicking my legs. As I did I thought about all the things that had happened to lead me to now.

So much of my life had been turned upside down but I wouldn't have had it any other way. I was happier now than I'd ever been, present situation not included. Finding out I was the descendant of a great elven warrioress had given me a purpose and something to fight for. Before then, I'd just been me, my only focus trying to make enough money to survive.

As I looked up again, I noticed the shore was finally a bit nearer. I might be tired but I just needed to keep going a bit longer.

The agents are finally dispersing. Zephyr's comforting voice appeared in my head. *I'm going to find somewhere on the ground to watch for a bit.*

I thought I could hear the tiredness in his voice as well and was grateful he was also going to get a break. It had clearly been a foolish idea to think that Zephyr and I could walk around in the middle of a busy place like LA and not be seen by somebody.

Minutes continued to tick by, and I had to pause again for a moment and let the ache disperse from my limbs. The next time I started up again, it felt like it was a little easier, and I wondered if the tide had finally turned.

It was a welcome relief when I could finally feel the sand underneath my toes again and put my feet down. For a moment I stood, buffeted about by the waves but no longer having to swim.

Minsheng went a little bit farther before putting his feet down and gaining stability but he too seemed to appreciate a break, looking to the shore with eyes full of longing.

Together, without either of us saying anything, we slowly walked to shore. As the height of the water on my torso fell, I began to feel self-conscious again, aware I was only wearing my underwear. I almost instinctively crouched lower, keeping the water level higher on my body and more of me shielded. But even if I had been bolder, Minsheng never looked my way.

When I could hide in the water no longer, I hurried to the edge and began unwrapping my parcel. It was slightly damp in places, where the water had splashed anyway, especially as we came through the breaking waves. The wind blew hard and goosebumps broke out all over my body. Before I could even get my t-shirt on I was shivering hard.

I pulled on my pants next, getting some sand inside them but not caring at all as they shielded me from the wind. Holding my shoes and socks in one hand I then walked up the beach. There were no agents in sight but I was still wary.

We're out of the water, I tried to project to Zephyr. *Where are you?*

On the roof of a cafe. I see you, but there are still agents lingering. The new guy thinks you must be around here somewhere, and has made his men wait at key locations.

Can we get to Daisy and Chris?

I think you can. I'm not sure I can.

Why not?

There is an agent right by the building I'm perched on. He pulled up here after I landed.

"Zephyr's stuck," I told Minsheng, relaying the information that the dragon had given me.

"Sounds like he needs a bit of a distraction."

I sighed, exhausted. But then I looked at Newton as he clambered down from Minsheng's shoulders onto the ground and frolicked in the sand. He was such a baby, and we'd already put him through so much. We needed to get him back to his family, and for that we needed Zephyr.

"I've got an idea," Minsheng said a moment later. "But it might involve a little thievery."

I grinned. It wouldn't be the first time I'd resorted to thievery. As long as whatever we took was replaceable or something we could pay for later, I could live with it.

CHAPTER TWELVE

As I helped Minsheng gather up all the different supplies he'd asked for, I couldn't help but wonder what it was he was creating. He'd taken a trash can on wheels, some rope from a nearby boat, and now he wanted a parasol as well.

Thankfully a local cafe had some parasols tied up by the back door. I handed him one as I looked at the construction.

He tied it on sideways, the top only partially open and stuck out to the front of the construction. And then he started sticking things on the other end.

"Reckon it looks a bit like a dragon?" he asked.

I lifted an eyebrow, not sure it did at all, but willing to bet an agent who saw it from afar would be distracted enough by it Zephyr would at least be able to get down from the roof.

"Do you think you can use your air control to move it along where you want it?" He grinned, clearly hoping the answer would be yes.

There was only one way to find out. I concentrated,

drawing in the air around me and imagining it going into the umbrella and pushing the wheel-based monstrosity along. At first it barely moved, but as it started to roll it gained momentum.

It wasn't very easy to steer, and it made a fair bit of noise but it was rolling along. With no brakes, I almost missed the turning past the cafe and down the street Zephyr had assured me contained an agent.

Running to the corner, I kept my eye on the distraction, and kept it going down the road, but not too close to the car the agent sat in. At first, I thought the agent must have seen past the ruse because nothing happened. But eventually, as I moved the creation down another road out of his sight, he got out and went to follow.

After giving it one final big push, I ran back to the other side of the cafe.

The coast is clear, I told Zephyr. A moment later the black outline of his flying shape appeared above me and then he landed beside me. I wrapped my arms around his neck and hugged him. Tears pricked the back of my eyes, and I had to fight them back. This wasn't a good time to cry.

I didn't like being apart from him, and given the way he nuzzled me as I pulled back, I was pretty sure he didn't like being apart from me either.

"Come on," Minsheng said. "Let's get out of here."

"I still think we should get Newton back to his family," I said.

Zephyr nodded, making it clear he felt the same way. A moment later Newton ran up and Zephyr lowered his leg and front left shoulder to let Newton climb up onto his back.

He's exhausted too, Zephyr explained.

It only made me more determined to get him back.

If Minsheng wanted to argue, he didn't even bother trying. Instead, all of us hurried back down the beach.

Where are the other agents? I asked Zephyr.

They spread out. We should be able to get to Newton's family without any of them seeing us.

Good. Then I think we need to hide in the van for a while.

I plan to. It's way past our bedtime. Even our unusual bedtime.

I chuckled aloud, earning me a look from Minsheng. I didn't explain. I was just too tired to.

Although I usually loved coming to the beach with Zephyr, today I'd had enough of it. I'd had enough of the sand, and I'd had enough of being out in the dark.

Thankfully, there didn't appear to be anyone else around, and it didn't take us long to get back to the part of the beach where Zephyr had said Newton's family would try to meet up with him.

Along the way, Minsheng sent Daisy and Chris another message. No doubt they would be wondering where we were and if we were okay.

"Daisy asked if we needed help, but I told her to stay put," Minsheng said as we reached the area we'd first started to look for Newton's family.

Up on the left, Zephyr said in my head as I began to slow.

He led the way, Newton beginning to get excited and chatter slightly. It had clearly been one heck of a rollercoaster for him. Especially as he probably didn't know if he could trust us fully.

Ahead, a small boathouse came into view. It looked a little run down and like it hadn't been used for several years. No wonder the fire salamanders thought this was a good place to meet up.

As we came closer, I looked around. There was no sign of any more of the creatures. Despite that, Newton ran down Zephyr's leg and up to the building. He appeared to be sort of sniffing around it, sticking out his tongue and searching.

A moment later, he disappeared into the building through a slight gap in one door. I crouched down to see if I could spot him inside, but the interior was too dark.

"What now?" I asked Minsheng. "Do you think he's safe in there?"

No sooner had I asked this when the fire salamander came shooting out and made several croaking noises at Zephyr.

They're gone. Zephyr's voice boomed in my head, the dragon already looking this way and that and letting out a little roar at Newton. *Something's happened to the others.*

I scooped Newton up.

"Don't worry," I said. "We'll find them."

I thought you said they were here earlier, I said to Zephyr as Newton snuggled against my chest and croaked some more.

They were.

Instantly my blood ran cold. If they went missing during the time we'd been evading the agents there was only one possible explanation. Instead of taking Newton to his family, we'd led the agents to them.

"What's going on?" Minsheng demanded as Zephyr started running down the nearest street and I jogged after him.

"The agents have taken the other fire salamanders," I said, hoping Zephyr knew what he was doing.

Thankfully the dragon stopped and slowed when he got to a road parallel to the beach, and hunkered down behind a bush.

We're in time, he informed me as I ran to his side and crouched to peek around too. I saw the two black sedans parked a little way up the road. Under the streetlight, an agent was loading a crate into a trunk already full of crates. Another agent was standing nearby, keeping a lookout and talking on a radio.

"We've got to help them," I said. "It's our fault."

"They want to take you in as well. If they call for backup you could get yourselves caught as well," Minsheng said. "There's such a thing as knowing when to run."

"I know, but we brought the agents to them and I can't just sit and watch."

Without waiting for Minsheng to respond or anyone else to try to come up with some kind of plan, I put Newton on my shoulder and drew in the energy and air I needed. Less than a second later I unleashed it, hitting both agents as hard as I could. As I blasted them, I got up and ran, my hands outstretched and keeping the pressure on. Both agents were knocked over, not expecting the assault, but they quickly tried to recover.

Fighting back against the force of my blast, they tried to get to their feet and reach for their weapons. But Zephyr had also come with me. He flew over my head, able to get to the men faster and exhale his gas down at street level. Stopping my blast so it wouldn't blow away the paralyzing gas, I ducked behind a car as one of them reached for his gun.

A dart broke the side window of the nearest car, setting off the car alarm.

Great. More attention. Just what we needed.

I peeked out to see that one of the agents had succumbed to Zephyr's gas, now lying on the road with his radio pressed up against his ear and unable to move. The other fired again as I pulled back, the dart hitting the wheel this time and making it hiss with escaping air. Newton let out a high-pitched sort of *rawr*.

"You and me both," I said, assuming he was expressing his annoyance at being fired at.

Pulling in more air and energy, I reached out to jet air at the agent's gun and disarm him, but he wasn't where he'd been moments earlier.

Gritting my teeth with frustration, I tried to see where he might have gone.

He's coming down behind the cars to your left, Zephyr said, flying over again. The dragon banked to one side as the agent fired again, and I could only assume he had shot up at the dragon.

Before I could move to the other side of the car I hid behind, I heard another shot. It was followed a little while later by the clatter of a gun. When I looked out I saw the agent was down, a dart in his back, and Daisy was standing there, a tranquilizer gun in one hand and one of the agents' radios in the other.

"Quickly," she said. "More agents are on the way. The other guy in the street managed to report your whereabouts before Zephyr got him with the gas."

"Of course he did," I replied, getting to my feet and rushing over to the dart gun. I grabbed it and tried to feel around for some more ammo and adrenaline shots. He'd fallen on the case as he'd gone down, this guy keeping it in a front pocket of his suit jacket. Thankfully none of the darts or the adrenaline syringe had broken, the case that held them pretty robust.

I shoved them in a pocket and then jogged over to the sedan with the open trunk. The second Newton saw his family, he let out many happy croaking noises, and they did the same, frantically trying to get out of the cages that held them.

When Zephyr had said that Newton had a family, I'd been thinking of a mom, dad, and a few siblings. Before me were at least ten different-sized fire salamanders. The largest pair were in a cage by themselves, both of them about three feet long each. I yanked open the hatch on their cage first. Next I chose one with a slightly darker-looking fire salamander in it and some smaller ones just like Newton.

The other two cages, including the one the agent had been in the middle of trying to load when I'd hit them, contained a handful of smaller salamanders each, some bigger than others, but all bearing similar markings on their backs.

Daisy and I helped them all down out of the trunk,

noticing how the first two were acting as shepherds for the rest, and then we all ran down the road back toward the junction and the route to the beach.

We've got company, Zephyr said a moment later before swooping overhead. I looked up to see him bank and turn toward the nearby roads, putting the beach behind him, and then he was out of sight again.

"You all need to get somewhere safe," I said to the salamanders, hoping they could understand me. For a moment Newton hesitated and I reached out to stroke him, then as one they scurried off into the night.

"Chris has the van a few blocks over that way," Daisy said, pointing northeast. "We just need to get to him."

As Daisy said this, she handed Minsheng the other gun she'd taken.

"Lead the way," he said. "But we need to make sure we're not followed."

"We can't afford for the agents to see the van," I explained as Daisy opened her mouth to question the statement.

A moment later she nodded, and then we set off.

Stay fairly close, I told Zephyr.

As close as I can.

I knew it didn't really need saying and Zephyr would do his best, but a part of me couldn't bear to have him a long way away from me again after being out in the ocean for so long while he was stuck somewhere else. The other part of me wanted to help keep him safe. And I knew he was likely to feel the same. I'd said it anyway. Sometimes you just had to.

We only managed to get a single block closer when

several sedans appeared. We ducked behind cars, and Zephyr landed in a front yard near us. I couldn't be sure they'd seen us as the cars slowly came closer, but Daisy's radio came to life a moment later.

"Men down," a voice said. "I've got two agents down, and it looks like someone freed the cargo."

"Roger that," another replied, this time the familiar voice of Agent Knox. "We've got the area surrounded again. They won't get past us this time."

I frowned, once again in the center of a field of agents I didn't know how to get out of and too far from Zephyr to feel comfortable.

We needed a new plan, and this time, it had to be a good one.

"It's only an hour until it will start getting lighter again," Minsheng said, his voice low and quiet. "We need to be out of here by then."

I nodded, wondering if he was about to suggest an idea or if he was merely expressing his concerns. When silence followed, I assumed it had been the latter. But that left us surrounded by agents, on the clock and with very little to aid us.

With Zephyr on the ground we also had no idea how many agents there were. Could we handle them, like we had the last two? Or were there far too many for us to just attack?

There was no way to know, but we needed to do something. And fast.

CHAPTER THIRTEEN

"What if we pretended to be an agent?" Daisy said, still listening to the agents' radio. I looked at Minsheng. He was the only one who could do so.

Sighing, he took the radio from her, then he looked both ways down the street and got a clock on the street name. We were between avenues Nine and Ten.

"We've got a sighting down on Avenue Eight," Minsheng said, trying to mimic the accent of one of the agents who had spoken earlier. "Requesting backup."

"On my way," someone replied, but we had no way of knowing who.

"Engage with caution," Agent Knox said. "Reminder that the girl can manipulate the air and the flying menace breathes some kind of paralyzing gas."

"Noted," Minsheng replied.

For a moment there was silence, and the agent in the sedan closest to us didn't move.

"Not seeing anything on Eighth," a voice said a moment later.

"Hell. They're not buying it," I said in response, but Minsheng held his hand up for silence.

"They're heading down to Seventh. The dragon looks to be injured, but an RV has pulled up. Request immediate assistance sealing off the area."

This seemed to have more of an effect. The sedan I could just see the edge of lit up its headlights and its engine started. A moment later, the agent pulled back onto the street and started driving down it.

"Still not seeing anything," the closest agent replied.

"In pursuit, down to Sixth now," Minsheng replied.

"Agent, identify yourself," Knox replied.

Minsheng hesitated, and the car heading away from us slowed and stopped again.

"Time to make a run for it," he said as he handed the radio back to Daisy. "Don't think I can buy us any more space."

Completely in agreement, I got to my feet and ran in the opposite direction down the road.

"Targets spotted," the radio squawked as we ran. At the same time the car the nearby agents were in reversed up the street and Zephyr leaped out of the yard and into the air.

My shoulders tensed as once more we were on the run, desperately trying to get away from the agents to somewhere safe. There were just too many of them and not enough defenses in our favor to win a battle today.

As the sound of gunfire came from behind us, I heard Minsheng grunt. He lifted his arm and pulled out a dart, but to my surprise, he kept running.

When I reached the corner of the road, Zephyr flying

above, I grabbed the low brick wall that bordered the front garden of the nearest house and used my momentum to turn and come down behind it. Crouching with the gun I held just above the wall, I steadied it, took aim at the agents coming our way, and fired.

I managed to hit one before the other opened fire back and another car screeched up the road.

"Go," I said to the others as they hesitated.

Minsheng still didn't move but Daisy and Zephyr both continued on. Only as I sprinted down the road again too did Minsheng move.

"Feeling sleepy yet?" I asked, concerned about the tranq dart as he finally pulled it out of his arm.

"A little, but we suspected the dwarven blood might be as similarly resistant as your elven blood."

"But Daisy was knocked right out last time," I replied between pants for air. It wasn't a great time to be discussing something like this, but I needed to understand.

"Although our father was part dwarf, and far more obviously than either of us, with how DNA works he clearly passed more dwarven elements on to me."

"Including resistance to some stuff," I finished for him.

"It would appear so," Minsheng said, ducking as more shots rang out. I glanced back to see the group of now three agents chasing us. They weren't any closer but all three carried dart guns. It was only a matter of time before one of us was hit again.

As I spotted another good place to stop and take a shot beside a low-slung sports car on the road a few yards in front of us, another black sedan came screeching around the corner ahead and turned in our direction.

Frelling crapsicles.

Do I even want to know what one of those is? Zephyr asked a moment later, banking as the agents shot at him too.

I held my breath, terrified they'd hit him, but he managed to dodge. Right overhead of the new car, Zephyr folded his wings and plummeted toward the agents as they got out.

Fighting back a scream, I watched as he fell, not entirely sure it was deliberate. When he was getting close to the agents who'd both tried to duck back into the car again, Zephyr exhaled. At the same time his wings unfolded and with one strong downbeat he slowed enough to land on the top of the car with a thud. Both agents now half in and half out of the car inhaled Zephyr's gas and became rigid.

The other agents shot at him, a dart catching him on the back before he could launch into the air again. I shot back, hitting another agent in the shoulder. I tried to run to Zephyr but more darts came my way, taking out the sports car's wing mirror not too far from my head.

Zephyr, you okay? I asked my companion as he continued to flap. He'd taken a dart but didn't seem to be showing any adverse effects.

I believe so. That weapon is strange. I don't feel as tired as it made me feel the last time they shot me with one, but it's harder to fly and move.

You're a lot bigger than the last time they shot you. It's clearly not strong enough anymore.

Perhaps, but I don't think I could take many more hits. I'm going to need to be more careful.

I'll distract them, I said, but I knew I was going to need a clear run and no one else to worry about. At the moment

Minsheng and Daisy were too close to me for me to draw the agents' fire and not just risk another one of us getting hit and sedated.

"Go," I said to Minsheng again as he and Daisy tried to get even closer and shoot too. "We've got this."

Minsheng opened his mouth to protest again, but I shoved him.

"You can't afford to take another hit, and they're focusing on Zephyr anyway. Go get the van ready."

This time he listened and gave me his spare ammo, his eyes saying what his words couldn't. He wanted me to be careful.

I continued to fire, drawing the remaining two agents' attention while Minsheng and Daisy hurried up the street. More of the sports car was chipped and dented, and I had the smug satisfaction of knowing that the agency was probably going to have to pay for all the damage when this was over, whether they caught me or not.

While the two agents were shooting me, yet another car pulled up behind them. I growled my frustration, the gun I carried out of ammo as well.

Ducking back behind the car, I quickly tried to reload. As I did I heard Zephyr roar. There were more shots, and then Zephyr grunted.

You okay? I asked, my hands shaking too much and dropping one of the darts.

Need to land.

Fear gripped at my heart, squeezing it in a vice that made it hard to breathe. With only a half-loaded gun, I emerged from my hiding place and shot straight at the nearest agent I saw. I was just too slow, and a dart thudded into my own chest, the sting extra painful.

As my racing heart pumped the sedative quickly through me, I felt my knees give, my eyes only just taking in feathers in the neck of the agent too.

Shitsticks. Frelling shitsticks, I thought, trying to fight, knowing I needed to stay awake but not sure I could. I drew on the air around me, pulling it in to me as a panicked attempt to hit back and clear everything around, but I couldn't concentrate hard enough.

I bit down on my own lip, the pain momentarily enough to keep me from slipping into oblivion, but it only lasted a few seconds before an agent appeared above me. At some point I'd laid myself down on the ground, but I couldn't remember when, only that the sky was beginning to grow lighter, the stars less bright, and the agent in front of me wore a smug grin I'd have loved to wipe off his face.

Aella! a deep voice boomed in my head. A moment later I felt the downbeat of wings as Zephyr appeared over me, exhaling gas. I did my best to use my magic and push the cloud away from me and toward the agent.

Before Zephyr could attack and I could do anything else but lay there, there was a loud bang and not only was Zephyr caught in another net, but I was as well, his body still partially over me.

Roaring his anger, Zephyr tried to leap away from me, and at least free me, but the net weighed him down too much.

Calm, Zephyr, I thought, closing my eyes for a moment, unable to keep them open any longer.

Don't go to sleep, he replied, his voice almost panicked.

At first it felt like he was a long way away. *Aella, you can't go to sleep. The agents are coming. He's coming.*

Which he? I thought, but a part of me knew. Agent Knox. I couldn't let Agent Knox take us.

But my body was so tired.

"Finally... The two rats caught in one trap."

Aella! Zephyr's voice screamed in my head. I felt his claws buffet my side, trying to roll me off my back, but I still didn't want to open my eyes.

A moment later a strange sort of pain began in the center of my chest and radiated outward. At the same time Zephyr let out a wounded roar. It shot adrenaline through me, bringing me back to the present.

My eyes flew open to see Agent Knox twisting something on Zephyr's back. I pulled air in as fast as I could, pausing for only a second to jet it at him as hard as I could, still dragging in more. He flew backward, knocked clear off his feet.

He smacked into the car behind with a crunch that no doubt would leave a dent.

"Get off my dragon," I said, getting into a crouch, my head coming up by Zephyr's. The pain slowly receded, but I was more awake now, my body already processing the sedative, the adrenaline keeping my heart racing and my mind clearer.

I watched Agent Knox get back to his feet as other agents came closer. Despite knocking him over, we were still trapped and I knew I had to play this carefully. There was no way either of us would be able to dodge more tranquilizer darts. A part of me didn't understand why they hadn't fired already and knocked us out.

As Knox came closer again, he sneered. I watched, drawing in air still, building up the energy inside me until I felt like my hair ought to stand on end.

"No sign of the others," the agent to our left said.

"They'll be here somewhere. Keep looking. And be careful. They won't want to leave these two to us." Knox didn't take his eyes off me as he spoke and I didn't look anywhere else either. What was he up to? Why were we still sitting here in the middle of the road?

Knox crouched, bringing his eyes down to my level, the net the only thing between us.

"I want to know where those lizards are," he said, his voice still deeper, his words clipped.

"Long gone," I replied. "Good luck trying to find them now."

I couldn't know it was true, but I knew if I was a fire salamander mom and I'd just got my kid back and I'd just avoided being abducted in a shiny cage together with my whole family, I wouldn't stick around to raise the kids in this vicinity. We'd be looking for a much safer home somewhere far from here.

"No. They'll be around here somewhere. They don't like to run and hide. It's not in their nature. Silly, really. They're such intelligent creatures in every other respect, but they develop a tie to a particular location and then they defend it."

I tried not to let my emotions or thoughts show. It sounded like Knox had run into fire salamanders before. As if he knew their patterns of life and had tracked down, and probably captured, a family in the past.

And as I thought about it, was I any different truly?

Everyone liked to think they'd act in the best possible way when something happened. But until something actually happened to you, you couldn't know for sure. It was clear so far that I didn't like to run. Not if I thought a fight might make me safer in the long run. So would I run if my children were in danger? Or would I fight the agents?

I had no way of knowing. The fire salamanders weren't here, but how was I going to make the agent before me realize that I truly didn't know where the fire salamanders were now? And did I even want to? If he thought I didn't have a use anymore I might find myself shot with a sedative again.

"So, let's try that again," Agent Knox said, making it clear I had to hurry and decide how to play this situation. "Where are those disgusting animals?"

"Behind you," I replied, the snark coming out before I could stop myself. To make matters worse, Knox turned and looked under the car that now had a Knox-shaped dent in the driver's side door. I couldn't help but laugh, and I even thought I heard a deep rumble of Zephyr chuckling.

This didn't go down well.

As Knox turned again, he held out his hand to the nearest agent. The agent unholstered the dart gun and handed it over.

Shitsticks.

Before he could fire, however, something leaped at him from the car behind, hissing and making a strange sort of roaring noise. He dropped the gun as his clothes caught alight and the creature jumped down.

Only a fraction of a second later Newton appeared, scurrying under the sports car nearby, another fire salamander with him. They both started chomping down on the net, trying to break through it.

Reaching out, I grabbed a broken piece of mirror from the road and very carefully used it like a knife. Between the salamanders and me, I was free within a minute, and I hurried out from the net. As I turned to help Zephyr get out too, I noticed Knox and three agents had managed to put out the fires the other salamanders had started and were trying to shoot them as well, or grab them and tackle them.

One of the agents managed to grab a medium-size salamander as it sat on the top of a car, its back alight for a moment. Momma salamander was quickest to respond, though, biting the agent until both salamanders fell to the ground. The female let out a screech and all the salamanders took cover under the cars.

Furious at the level of force they were trying to use on the creatures just trying to defend themselves and us, I pelted all four agents with air, aiming for their guns, faces and any outreached hands before they could get to the salamanders.

Then I summoned up the largest amount of air I had the force for and hurled it at them, centered on Knox. All four were swept down the road, falling over. I kept advancing, pushing them along and into the ground, seeing red.

Aella, we're free, Zephyr's voice sounded in my head. *We all need to get out of here.*

At first I didn't stop. I'd had enough of being pushed around. But as Zephyr repeated the words and the men continued to be buffeted down the road, I eased off. More agents came running up, but I didn't stick around to find out whether they were going to attack us or help their friends. Instead, Zephyr and the rest of us all took off down the street.

With Zephyr able to fly, and the salamanders moving so fast they were almost a blur, I was the slowest of the group. Once again I used my abilities, but this time to help move myself along at a faster rate, the wind giving me extra forward momentum.

Next right. I see the van. Minsheng looks pretty pissed. Chris and Daisy are keeping him from coming to look for you.

I gulped, more scared of how cross he might be than I was of the agents right now. Despite that thought I kept walking, and soon we were all around the corner.

Thankfully the salamander family grabbed Minsheng's attention.

"They came back to help us out," I said as first Newton and then his family jumped into the back of the van. "We ran into some trouble and they stopped us getting overwhelmed."

Zephyr landed beside me, letting out a snort. He didn't admonish me for glossing over the truth, merely climbing into the back of the van as well.

"We'd best go before anyone sees us," Minsheng said, getting in and offering me a hand up.

As Daisy shut the doors and hid us from view, Chris pulled off.

I exhaled as I sank down, one hand resting on Zephyr. Exhaustion had never hit me so hard, and for a while I couldn't even speak. But we were safe, and no one had been taken by the agency. I was willing to consider that a win right now.

CHAPTER FOURTEEN

I yawned and stretched before opening my eyes. My whole body seemed to ache and I still had sand in places I definitely didn't want it, but Zephyr and I were still alive, and together.

The dragon was still asleep beside me, as were most of the fire salamanders. Minsheng smiled as I sat up. Daisy and Chris were nowhere to be seen.

When I noticed that Minsheng had one of his books open on his lap, I scooted over to see what he was reading. No doubt it would be something he thought might help us in our present situation.

After getting away from the agents that morning, Chris had found a quiet place to park and let everyone get some sleep. It was now at least afternoon, but I couldn't be sure when exactly.

Before I could say anything to Minsheng my stomach rumbled, making it clear I was starving.

"Daisy and Chris have gone to get us supplies again," Minsheng whispered.

"Wonderful," I replied as Newton stirred as well. He hopped up into my lap and cozied up.

Slowly stroking him, I sat back and looked at the book in Minsheng's hands. It was the one on Tuviel and Azargad. I'd looked at it several times, but Minsheng had already seemed to know it by heart.

"What are you looking for?" I asked. "Anything helpful?"

He flicked back to where he'd put his thumb to mark a page. It was one of the illustrated pages, where someone had drawn Tuviel and Azargad together in the air, the elven warrior riding on his back.

"It's the only picture I can find with that necklace in it," Minsheng said. "Near the end of their time together. But I can't find any mention of it. I know they have their secrets, and the organization does too, but I thought there would be some information somewhere on what that thing can do."

"Did Tuviel not say?"

"She lived a very long time ago. It's possible everyone then knew what it could do, but no one thought it was worth mentioning."

"It helps me and Zephyr talk to each other," I replied, not sure if that was the sort of thing Minsheng meant. I didn't know if it needed to do anything else. Being able to communicate with Zephyr, even if it was only in our minds, was the icing on the cake of the bond we already shared. I was already so used to it.

"I think it does more than enable telepathy. You've both been different since you put the necklace on. As if it enhances all elements of the bond between you both."

I nodded. It made sense. I'd been able to feel his presence so much more. And it turned out, I could feel his pain. We were more linked than I'd have thought possible.

"Although I trust the organization, I'm concerned too. Tuviel only gained it later in her journey. It doesn't say how long she lived afterward."

"Why am I sensing that there's a big *but* coming?" I asked, noticing several more of the salamanders wake up until just grandma salamander and Zephyr were still asleep.

"Tuviel and Azargad were defeated by someone incredibly powerful. Someone who used the extra strong bond between the pair to his advantage." Minsheng flicked back to the page he was on, read a few lines and then closed the book.

"Do you know anyone who might be able to tell us?" I asked. "Or could someone examine it? See if they can work out what the enchantments are?"

"Possibly, but they don't live in LA..." Minsheng sighed.

"What it does isn't the main thing bothering you though, is it?" I asked when he stared at the small bag full of his best books.

"No. It's how willing the organization was to give you something they didn't know was safe, simply because it would probably make you more powerful."

"Is that normal for them?" The organization was a topic I'd always wanted to ask more about. Minsheng mentioned them only when necessary though. And until now we'd not had a quiet moment since I'd put the necklace on.

"I..." Minsheng trailed off. "I don't think so, but in truth, I can't be sure."

Before I could ask any more, Daisy and Chris returned.

They carried bags of food between them, but not just food, they also had other important supplies like flashlights, a couple of blankets and even a small first-aid kit.

As the smell of a bacon and cheese bagel wafted through the air, Zephyr finally woke up and we all tucked in.

"There's agents in the area," Chris said. "Almost as if they knew we came this way but still can't find us. I don't think we should stay here any longer."

"If you think we can get there without being followed, we should go to the warehouse," I replied without missing a moment. "I want to know what you all think of it."

Minsheng lifted an eyebrow, but Chris just passed me the map on his phone and got me to enter in the coordinates. It took me a moment to find it, especially given that it was a garden on the map and not a building. Eventually, I thought I had it marked.

While Chris drove us through the LA traffic, I ate and thought. Maybe I could test the necklace I wore by taking it off and putting it on again. Or maybe what it did would all be subtle things like our bond growing stronger or us healing faster.

I never got a chance to try it, eating right up until we were near the building. Now we were close, Zephyr looked around himself as if he recognized the warehouse.

Chris went straight past the marker on his satnav for a couple of blocks and then turned right. Not long after that, he pulled up and looked at me.

"Anything we should know about this warehouse?" Chris asked.

I shrugged, not sure what kind of thing they'd want to

know. I'd already mentioned that it was where I'd found Zephyr and that it had been abandoned. It was Minsheng himself who had discovered that the warehouse had been sort of hidden my entire life.

"All right then," Chris said. "Let's go see what's inside."

He got out before anyone could object and started a tidal wave as we all crawled out of the cramped space. It was late evening, and this part of LA was quiet. Despite that, I was still wary about people spotting Zephyr. The last thing we wanted was to lead the agents to the warehouse before we had a chance to check it out completely and hide ourselves inside.

My head full of nervous thoughts and worries about their reaction to the building, I led the group back down the road and toward the alley where my mugger had led me.

No one said anything but I noticed Daisy raise her eyebrows when we reached the alley full of dumpsters. Biting my lip, I walked down the side of the building toward the door that had been open the first time I'd been there.

It stood open again, just like that night, although in the day it didn't look like quite so much of a refuge.

Walking inside, I went in just far enough that everyone else could follow. It smelt much the way it had the first time I was there, unused but not damp. And it was equally as empty.

"This is huge," Daisy said.

I looked her way and noticed she was grinning. Some of the tension left my shoulders.

Having broken the silence, this seemed to release an

unspoken restraint on everyone else. The salamanders began running around exploring the building and even Zephyr jumped into the air and flew around. I marveled at how much space he had to fly and how much better this was than the training room we had at Minsheng's restaurant.

I wished I'd thought of it sooner, but in my head the place had been dark, dreary and nowhere near as big as this. It didn't help that the last time I'd been here I'd been frightened and investigating a strange glow all by myself. Walking into the building with friends, a dragon and my newfound abilities, I wasn't scared at all.

"This definitely looks like a useful building. It's hard to believe that this has just stood here unused for all these years." Minsheng turned on the spot, taking it all in.

"It's a better place to hide than we've found so far," I replied.

He nodded, smiled and patted me on the shoulder.

"I'll go tell the organization the good news. Maybe they can lease it for us."

Minsheng's words made a warm feeling grow in the pit of my stomach and fill my chest. Since I'd met him and he'd helped me get away from the agents the first time, I'd been relying entirely on him. I'd gone where he'd suggested and I'd taken the precautions that he'd recommended... with very few exceptions.

It had been clear from the beginning that he cared about my safety, despite my ridiculous propensity to often get in trouble. It felt good to have a solution to the problem of keeping us all safe. A solution that he didn't disapprove of.

"And this is where you found Zephyr?" Daisy asked. "How did you even know to look inside?"

"You could sort of say I was led here," I replied. "Do you want to see where I found him?"

"I think we'd all like to know where on earth in here you'd hide a dragon egg," Chris replied for her.

Grinning even more, I led them to the stairs at the opposite end of the building. It didn't take us long to climb, especially when I wasn't being anywhere near as cautious as I had been the last time I was there.

In the dusk, the room above seemed far bigger, the three cordoned off areas clearly supposed to be offices.

I walked slowly to the middle one, picturing the night I'd found Zephyr's egg.

"Here," I said, pointing at the corner of the middle cubicle. "His egg was sitting in the wooden basket just in the corner here."

As I said these words Zephyr came in through the doorway, flying in and landing in a move I'd never seen him do before. He came over to me as if he'd heard my words, his head nuzzling against my arm.

"The egg was glowing when I first arrived. At least, I think it was glowing. I could see a green light from outside by the door we came in, and as I got closer it got dimmer and dimmer until it had faded to just the egg. A glowing greenish-brown egg."

"Glowing, like it knew you were coming? Like it knew you were close?" Daisy asked.

I shrugged. Minsheng had wondered if at some point I'd bonded with the egg before I could even remember, but if that was true, then that meant someone had planned for me to be there that day.

It made me think back to the man who'd mugged me. He'd had a face similar to Chris', a face that I now knew came from a gnome. But he'd clearly been after my hairbrush. Could he also have been leading me here? I had no way of knowing, and I didn't voice my thoughts.

It was bad enough that someone had left Zephyr there for me to find and hidden the building from all records and all maps. I didn't want to think about who was that powerful and why they had orchestrated my life the way they had.

"Looks like the building carries on this way," Daisy said, her voice coming from somewhere to the left. "There's some stairs back down again."

More than a little curious, and grateful I hadn't realized that there was more to the building the last time I'd been here, I went to see what she meant. Just past the leftmost cubicle was a more open area, where the light could stream in from the front of the building and the lamp posts outside.

At the far end in the corner was a set of double doors. Daisy stood between them, having clearly pulled them open. I went to her side and saw the view she had, a set of stairs that swept back downwards.

This area of the building was dusty and smelt like it had been more closed up. It was clear no one had been here in a long time.

As we descended I noticed we were coming toward a sort of reception area. The glass that would have once been an open, inviting area was now boarded up, but it was clear these were supposed to be the front doors. A reception area sat to one side, with room for sofas or chairs and a small waiting room opposite. On the other side of the double front doors were toilets and a large kitchen.

As Chris followed us down the stairs, and Daisy went into the kitchen to see what was in there, I noticed another small corridor that ran down the side. I followed it, Zephyr coming with me, his presence a comforting warmth.

As I reached the end of the corridor, it took a turn to the right, back toward the main area of the warehouse, but instead of joining up with it, it was blocked off. I approached, noticing that there was a slight difference in the color of the bricks in the middle section of the wall. At some point someone had removed the door and bricked it up to make it match the rest of the building.

Having no explanation as to why, I went back toward the kitchen and found both Chris and Daisy excitedly pulling unused pots and pans, most of them a little dusty, out of the cupboards.

"This whole kitchen, this whole warehouse, it's like someone set it up for us to use already." Daisy pulled out a set of cooking utensils to make a point.

"Looks like I'd better start making a shopping list then," Chris said as he pulled out a piece of paper and a pen. "Going to need some sturdy locks, food, and a little bit of furniture."

"We can use the office space upstairs as bedrooms," Daisy said. "If we get some curtain rails or something, we could even make them a bit more private."

Chris nodded as he continued to add things to his list. For a moment I couldn't talk. This place felt like it might be able to become our home. And hearing Daisy's excitement as she planned furniture for us and ways to make it feel comfortable only made me feel more relieved.

With all the guilt I'd felt at seeing Minsheng's restaurant being trashed by the agents for a second time, some of the damage even having come from my own abilities as I tried to defend us, I felt intense relief. Knowing that this place was far more robust and would have no other use than to train would make it easier to defend if the agents did show up. I felt so much lighter I thought I might float off if someone removed the roof, an enormous weight gone from my shoulders.

Going back up the stairs, I went straight to the middle cubicle and put my stuff down. For now, this would be my room, mine and Zephyr's. It seemed fitting that we would live where we'd found each other.

CHAPTER FIFTEEN

Laughing, I watched Zephyr playing a game a bit like tag with the salamanders on the main warehouse floor. I stood watching from the top of the steps into the other section of the building. Behind me, Chris and Daisy were measuring up the office space and working out what furniture we would want to get first. We'd already decided that it wasn't worth getting full beds, just air mattresses first, and instead get things like sofas and a small table.

I tried not to think about how much it would all cost, hoping the organization would pay for it. But as Minsheng reappeared, coming back into the warehouse from outside, the serious expression on his face said it all. I hurried downstairs to meet him, wondering what the organization must have said.

"You still don't know who your actual parents are?" Minsheng asked as he came closer. "Do you?"

I was too stunned by the sudden blunt question to know exactly how to reply. He sighed and ran a hand through his hair.

153

"I'm sorry. That wasn't very kind of me."

"The organization has a problem with us being here, don't they?" I asked. Minsheng nodded.

"In truth, I agree with them, at least a little. They're concerned that whoever has been hiding this warehouse might not be a friendly entity. By trying to lease the building, we reveal ourselves to them."

"Is that their only objection?" I asked as I folded my arms across my chest.

"Not their only one, but the strongest, and the one that makes the most sense." Minsheng sighed again as if there had been others that he disagreed with.

"Then why don't we just stay here without leasing it officially? Isn't there like some law that if we squat here for long enough and no one throws us out the building practically belongs to us anyway?"

"Yup," Chris said, his voice coming from above and behind. I turned to see him standing at the top of the stairs. "Squatters have rights."

"The organization is still very keen for us to go and join the Sanctuary rather than trying to take on the agents in LA and antagonize them even further."

"And you think that's the safer option as well? It probably is the safer option," I said, deciding to be honest. "But I still won't do it. I understand if any of you want to go, but I spent my whole life running away. I never faced my problems in the past, but I know who I am now. And I'm a lot more powerful than I was before. If I don't take a stand somewhere, I'm going to be running for the rest of my life."

"Sometimes, running away is the right thing to do. It's

not always a bad thing to get out of the situation or a fight that you can't win and come back when you're stronger."

I nodded, but it still didn't change anything.

"I'm staying here, and I'm going to work out how to deal with these new agents. I'd like it if you helped me, but I'd understand if you didn't. I'm going to protect Zephyr and the fire salamanders and any other mythical creature we come across between now and driving out the agency. And I'm going to do it from this building."

"I'm not going to waste my breath trying to argue with you. Whether I agree with you or not, if you truly won't leave, I will stay and help you. But Aella, you're not strong enough yet. We're not strong enough yet. Not to beat the agency. Not with the level of technology and resources they currently have."

"We'd best get training then, and figuring out how we can beat them." I started walking back to the offices and the stairs up to them, feeling cross and indignant at being told I was wrong and I was taking the wrong course of action. It wasn't going to change my mind, however.

"It's going to take more than training," Minsheng called after me.

"I'd best start getting the supplies we need, especially those locks then," Chris replied as I stormed past him.

"I'll come help," Daisy added, hurrying off to him and clearly not wanting to be in the building while I and Minsheng were having such a disagreement.

This only made me feel even more cross, and I stomped all the way up to the cubicle I had decided was my bedroom. Flopping down on the floor, I exhaled and tried to calm myself down. It wasn't entirely Minsheng's fault. I had to keep reminding myself that he really did want what was best for me, and that he was just trying to keep me and Zephyr safe from forces in this world that none of us entirely understood.

While I sat there thinking about the agency and the threat they represented, my hands instinctively reached for my bag and pulled out the transceiver that would let me know what was happening in the agents' headquarters. There had been a burst of activity earlier that day so I made myself a bit more comfy and pressed play.

"Please tell me that having half my team working on scrubbing photos from laptops and phones and having to offer payments for damaged vehicles and car alarms going off in the early hours of the morning has all been worth it," Crawley said, clearly more than a little pissed off.

"I swear, that little brat seemed to know causing more damage meant more of an outlay for us," Knox replied.

"So where is the little brat now?"

There was silence. The kind of silence that could stop a moving ship just as effectively as an iceberg could. The kind of silence that carried an atmosphere with it so thick that even I could feel it on the other end of the recording.

I grinned, knowing what Knox was going to have to say next.

"I won't ask again, dammit. Where are they?" Crawley asked, a bang following her statement. I imagined her slamming the desk with her fist.

"I don't know," Knox replied. The smile on my face grew even wider.

"What do you mean, you don't know? You'd better start explaining."

"That family of fire salamanders—they attacked us. The moment we had both the girl and the dragon pinned down under a net. Neither of them could do a damn thing to stop us. And then a swarm of angry fire salamanders mobbed us. By the time we bested them, she'd cut them loose and they'd run."

"Then at least tell me you got the damn fire salamanders."

More silence. I tried to imagine Knox's face. Would he look ashamed? Or would he keep that slightly haughty I-know-what-I'm-doing look?

"And how am I going to explain this one to Jacobs?"

"You won't have to," Knox replied. A moment later there was the sound of a scrape of a chair across the hard floor. I could only assume that Knox had gotten up.

"And why is that?"

"Because I'll find her and that dragon. And every single little fire salamander and despicable creature that helped her. And I'll bring them all in by the end of the day."

"You had better. But if Jacobs calls and asks me how everything is going, I'm going to tell him exactly what is happening. That you have come here, and stirred a hornets' nest, causing untold amounts of damage and running amok in LA in public in broad daylight, and you have nothing to show for it. And if anything, you have made the dragon and the girl even harder to catch."

"If I'd had all the information at the beginning, this wouldn't have gotten so bad. But you let her find more allies. Wasn't just one fire salamander, it was a whole family of them."

"Do you think Jacobs will care about that? When you

said you had loads of experience dealing with all sorts of creatures? No, Knox, you're not going to blame me for this one."

There was more silence followed by the slam of the door. A moment later another chair scraped along the floor and the sound of someone tapping away at keys on a computer reached my ears. I switched off the transceiver, more than a little relieved.

For now, they didn't know where we were and they didn't know how to get us. Even with Knox trying his best, as long as I, Zephyr and the fire salamanders stayed inside the warehouse, they weren't going to find us.

Not long after I switched it off, Minsheng appeared and sat down only a yard or so away from me.

"If we're going to have any chance of beating them and getting them to leave us alone again, we're going to need to come up with a plan," he said.

"I'm sure between us we can come up with something." I nodded and smiled, glad we weren't at odds any more.

Before we could do anything else, however, Newton appeared, rushing in from the main warehouse and making a lot of noise. I got up, going over to him, but he just darted back the way he'd come. Heading down the stairs, I tried to follow as fast as he moved, but I could barely keep up.

As I got to the bottom I noticed all of his family were by the door, swirling back and forth and making a strange hissing sort of noise. Zephyr swept back and forth above, a silent sentinel who couldn't be seen from outside.

"What is it?" I asked as I jogged closer, almost instinctively pulling in the air around me in case I needed to defend them.

As I opened the door and stepped outside, I noticed a delivery driver, a box in his hands.

"Aella-Faye?" he asked, watching the salamanders behind me with wide eyes.

I didn't confirm it, but I moved closer, the salamanders staying close to me.

"It's okay, Newton. Not a threat," I finally said when they hissed more as he tried to pass me the box.

"Sorry," I added as I took it and he asked me to sign on a device. "They're not used to the place yet. Makes them more defensive. They won't hurt you."

He nodded like he didn't believe me and stepped back a little again. With no idea who the box was from and aware that incredibly few people knew I was in the warehouse, I didn't sign with the usual signature, instead scribbling Tuviel instinctively.

The guy didn't even check my signature, backing away as soon as he had his device back. I carried the box farther into the warehouse staring at the topmost label on it. Who had known I was here? More importantly, why so many labels on the box? It looked like it had not only traveled all over the country, but this wasn't the first time its delivery to the warehouse had been attempted.

Zephyr landed beside me, his eyes on the package as well. Neither of us needed to say a word as I climbed up the stairs, holding the box ahead of me like it might explode at any moment.

"I'm not sure you should be the one opening that,"

Minsheng said as I put it down on the office floor and explained what had happened.

"Be my guest," I replied, although a part of me was scared for him too.

Pulling out a pen knife, I offered it to him. He flicked the blade out and cut the tape in a few clean slices before giving it back to me.

I moved so I was farther back but would still be able to see what was inside once he pulled the lid back. For a moment Minsheng didn't open it, looking between me and the parcel. It took all my self-control not to lean forward and open it anyway. I was only so patient, and more than a little curious.

Eventually, Minsheng reached down and opened the first tab. Before he could pull open the final tab, I leaned forward and looked down. Inside was a wooden box.

I gasped. The carvings on it matched the ones on the basket inside which I'd found Zephyr's egg.

As Minsheng reached in and pulled out the box I could only stand in awe, my mind reeling and full of questions.

"Does this match that box you had in your room?" Minsheng asked, clearly recognizing it too.

"Yes, I think so." I motioned for him to open it.

Cautiously, he lifted the lid of the box, it coming away as a separate piece revealing a lined interior. I marveled at the soft velvet inside but that wasn't what drew my eyes. There was an envelope. It was roughly the size of A4 paper and it had my name on it. On top of the envelope was a set of keys.

As Minsheng picked up the keys I reached forward and took the envelope. It wasn't sealed, just folded shut, so I pulled it open and withdrew the contents. It was a sheath of thick papers, the first also bearing my name.

It took me a moment to realize that I was looking at a certificate of ownership. Specifically, a deed declaring that I owned a building in this part of LA. I showed it to Minsheng, not quite sure what I was looking at.

"Does this mean the building we're standing in is owned by me?" I asked Minsheng. His eyes went wide as he scanned the piece of paper I was holding up.

"Yes. Yes, it does," Minsheng replied.

"But how?" I let him take it from me as I looked at everything else I held. Most of it appeared to be legal documents. Documents that confirmed I owned the building and what that meant. There were also mortgage documents declaring that someone had taken out the building in my name and paid the bills until it was completely paid off. I owned the building outright.

But the thing that drew my eyes the most and made me feel most stunned was the date on the document declaring the building mine. It was my official birth date. The day I'd been found on a police station doorstep. The day Minsheng had said that this warehouse had been declared unsafe for people to visit. The day it had been made off-limits to everybody.

Just as I'd suspected, someone had planned for me to be here. To find the building in the future and make use of it. But who? Was it my biological parents? Was someone else orchestrating my life?

I didn't know what to do, or how to feel. For a while I just stared at the pieces of paper in front of me, until Minsheng gently gathered them back up, putting the certificate of ownership back on top, and tucked them back in the envelope. He then handed me the keys.

"I won't pretend to understand how this must make you feel," Minsheng said. "But it definitely seems like whoever meant for you to find Zephyr also meant for you to have this building. I don't know if we really should stay or if the organization is right and we should go and try to find the Sanctuary, but this is definitely a blessing."

"Do you think it could be my parents, my real parents?" I asked. Almost immediately, tears pricked the back of my eyes, and I wondered if I was just clutching at straws, a hope I'd not felt in a long time flourishing in my chest.

"I don't know. If your parents could do all this, then why didn't they keep you? It doesn't make enough sense. I know it would be amazing if it was your parents. But I don't want to give you hope that I'm not sure will be fulfilled. Whoever this is, they don't seem to want to own their own actions. They're hiding in the shadows and they left you to defend yourself for over twenty years."

As I wiped my tears away, I sighed. Minsheng was right. Whoever these people were, whoever it was who wanted me to be in the warehouse, they could have done different things at a different time, and they definitely didn't seem like loving parents. The realization hit harder having hoped even for just a moment.

It was only as we were putting everything back inside the box that I realized they'd put my name on everything before I even had my name. I told Minsheng.

"I don't understand," he replied.

"When I was found on the police station doorstep, I didn't have a birth certificate. That meant I had no name.

My adopted parents named me a week or two later. They named me Aella-Faye. So how could this warehouse have been put in my name, Aella-Faye, the day I was left at the police station?"

"I have no idea. None of it makes any sense."

I didn't reply. I knew it was a lot to hope for, that Minsheng would be able to make some sense of it all or would have answers for me, but I felt even more disappointed knowing that he didn't.

Minsheng reached out and put a hand on my shoulder.

"Aella, I know this is hard. And I know you don't really feel like you belong anywhere. But I'm here now. And no matter what happens, I will stay with you. I spent my whole life waiting for you. We'll find a way through this together, I promise."

As more tears flowed down my face, I moved forward and hugged him. I was starting to suspect that home wasn't a place, but rather the people you were with.

CHAPTER SIXTEEN

A couple of hours later I was standing in the middle of the warehouse watching Zephyr give the younger fire salamanders a ride around on his back when Chris and Daisy returned. Not only did they walk through the open doorway, arms full of supplies, but behind them came another familiar face.

"Lyra!" I ran toward her as I spoke.

She laughed, and the two of us hugged.

"What are you doing here?" I asked as I pulled back and looked at her again.

"I bumped into these guys outside one of the dojos downtown. They were getting rid of a bunch of old matting, and some of the more worn-out equipment. I went down to see if there was anything good to pick up and found these guys already there claiming it."

"But they don't know you, and you didn't know them."

"Chris was telling the dojo about how he was about to use it all for a friend of his. Said you were phenomenal with nunchucks and down on your luck. That the very people who were supposed to be protecting you had chased you away from your old life. Then I think they mentioned something about you being an orphan."

"Chris. Aren't you supposed to be making it hard for people to find me, not easy?"

At this, Daisy laughed.

"I didn't tell them anything that would lead them to you, but all good lies have as much truth in them as possible. How was I to know that the people around me already knew who you were?" Chris shrugged.

"It's okay, Aella," Lyra replied. "Until I said that I knew you had a dragon and I knew the agency was after you, they didn't admit they knew you at all."

"I'm sorry I never got back to you." I bit my lip as I wondered what her reaction was going to be. After the agents had chased me from her apartment thanks to a call she'd made, I didn't dare contact her number and let her know anything about my new life.

"I've been worrying about you for two whole months! I mean, I know it was my fault. And I'm sorry that I led them to you. But when I heard Chris today, I had to ask. I had no idea if you were okay or not."

"They never managed to catch me, but it's been a wild ride," I replied as I grabbed the pile of supplies Daisy dropped by the door, noticing several bags of food. Lyra did the same, and the two of us walked toward the kitchen.

I filled her in on what had happened since I'd left her flat as we went back for a second load. While we moved the equipment farther into the warehouse, Chris and Daisy went back and forth from the van to add to the pile by the door. Along the way I introduced Lyra to Minsheng and the fire salamanders.

"Did you say fire salamanders?" she asked when Newton came up and sniffed her fingers.

"Yup, fire salamanders. They can literally start fires, but mostly they're just incredibly warm and can change colors like mood rings."

We paused for a moment as she introduced herself to the other salamanders when they came up. Within seconds she was stroking their heads and Newton had climbed up her, going a shade of deep blue.

By the time Chris and Daisy had gotten everything inside and Chris had moved the van back out of the way, there was a pile of building supplies by the door, air beds to pump up and various martial arts gear to begin making a new dojo.

"Sounds like you guys could do with a bit more help," Lyra said looking around the warehouse and frowning at how empty it was.

"You probably shouldn't stick around," I replied despite wishing she could. "The agency that is after me isn't going to stop, not unless I make them. And the guy in charge is pretty trigger-happy."

"They completely and utterly trashed my apartment. Broke a whole bunch of stuff, and they wrecked your old life. I'm happy to help, especially if you're going to teach them a lesson."

I grinned, definitely intending to do the latter.

"I'll go get some kind of dinner started then," Minsheng said. "Looks like we've got a lot of mouths to feed."

"I'll go get the rest of those mats and pads from the dojo." Daisy picked up the van keys as she spoke.

Without any words, Chris went over to the open door frame at the top of the stairs and began installing the door he'd bought.

"Want to help me set up our dojo?" I asked Lyra. Nodding and smiling, she grabbed the edge of the nearest mat and began dragging it to one side of the warehouse.

With something to focus on and an old friend to talk to, I soon forgot some of the difficulties of the last few days. We could have been setting up a dojo anywhere.

"Don't worry, I didn't bring my phone. Didn't want to risk the agents tracking me here and finding you again," Lyra said when we got back to the subject of what happened in her apartment the morning she'd left me and Zephyr in it. "I learned my lesson."

"You had no way of knowing that knowing even one person would bring them there so quickly," I replied.

"No, but I should have been more careful. I'm just glad you're all right. And you've got a lot of new friends."

Before either of us could say any more, Daisy arrived with another van load and Lyra went to help unload it.

By the time the dojo was complete, Minsheng had also finished cooking. We all made our way to the office space above and, sitting on air beds, cushions and anywhere else we thought looked comfortable, we all chowed down.

Several times I considered telling them all about the mysterious parcel that had arrived while they were out, but I couldn't quite bring myself to do so. For now, I wanted it to be secret. I didn't want their pity for being an orphan, and I definitely didn't want their curiosity and their questions about who my benefactor could be.

Instead, we talked about plans for the next few days. We needed an awful lot of stuff still. With none of us wanting to get anything delivered, we were going to need to keep the van for a while and use it to pick up furniture and more supplies for Chris and Minsheng to build a new training facility.

"Can you get some sand as well, please," I asked when Chris was making yet another list.

"Sand?" Chris blinked a few times as he stared at me.

"Yeah. We found a set of stairs that go up to the roof. The warehouse is tall enough that the flat area up there can be turned into a small recreation garden. The fire salamanders recharge sitting in the sand under the sun toward the end of the day. They can't go to the beach anymore, so I thought we could bring the beach to them."

"That's a wonderful idea," Daisy replied, beginning to grin. "Maybe we can even get a few deckchairs and a paddling pool at some point."

Her enthusiasm was infectious, and the whole group started talking about a way to turn the rooftop into a sort of garden. There was even talk of a barbecue.

All of it left me with a slight worry about how we'd pay for it all. As Lyra left and Daisy and Chris went back down to the warehouse floor to finish putting all the locks on the door and securing the downstairs for the night, I helped Minsheng wash up.

"If the organization doesn't approve of this idea, then I assume they're not paying for it either," I said as I stacked another dry plate back in the cupboard.

"Both Chris and I get wages from them, if that's what you're worried about."

"Yes, but no, not exactly. I clearly now have some assets. I should be the one paying for all this. But I can't just go get a job."

"I'm honestly surprised the organization hasn't offered to provide wages for you. I mentioned it would be the right thing to do when I told them the agency had taken everything from you."

"Oh," I replied, not sure what else to say to this news. I'd assumed all this time that the organization was some kind of benevolent force. I hadn't expected any wages from them, though. To know they'd decided not to award them to me when Minsheng thought they normally would have made me reassess what I knew about them.

"But a wage would likely come with a lot of strings, however. For starters, they'd probably insist on you leaving LA," Minsheng continued.

I stopped as I was about to open my mouth and declare the organization could shove their wages if that was the case. But I needed money and it didn't feel right to live off Minsheng and Chris. Minsheng had already lost a restaurant and Chris his van, and the two of them were happily spending even more of their money on fitting out this warehouse.

"You want to be paying your way, don't you?" Minsheng asked a moment later.

"Completely," I replied. "But I don't want to be forced to leave either. I'd get any kind of job to pay for what we needed if I didn't think the agency would show up the second I worked right now."

"Then consider some of my wages yours. The organization is paying me to train you and keep you safe. To help ensure that magic and mythical creatures aren't wiped from this world for good. If you train hard, and learn about your history and the animals we need to protect, then you'll be helping me do just that. I'll pay you, or pay for the things you need for you. That work?"

"I guess. But it means you'll be getting less." I picked up my tea towel and the next wet plate and kept drying.

"They gave me a raise when I started training you anyway. My job got more dangerous and more important. After all, you're one of the mythicals' best hopes right now."

I gulped, not sure how to respond to that. I was still just me. The runaway orphan who could barely afford to live and seemed to have been screwing up her life at regular intervals for as long as she could remember.

"Why don't we try out the new dojo after this?" Minsheng asked. "Your left uppercut is still a bit sloppy. Especially when you make it faster with your air boost. Or however you do that thing."

Glancing at Minsheng, I caught the sparkle in his eyes and the wry smile. Instantly, I felt grateful. He was giving me something to focus on. Something I could control. Becoming a better fighter in every way I could increased my chances of beating the agency. And I planned to stack the deck in my favor as much as possible.

As soon as we were in the dojo, Zephyr, the fire salamanders, Daisy, and Chris all came to watch. Lyra had gone back to hers with a promise to check in with us only if she could do so without the agents tailing her. As much as I wanted her around and we could have done with her help, I didn't doubt the agents would be keeping an eye on her.

I tried not to feel too self-conscious as Minsheng and I bowed to each other. I'd generally had an audience all the time during my previous lessons, but I knew there was more pressure on this. Before I'd found out who I was, the sensei was supposed to win, his skill and experience giving him the advantage in almost every element. With Minsheng I was supposed to be able to use my abilities to be faster and more accurate than him.

I struck first, barely getting any extra power behind it, but it still caught Minsheng off guard. He just managed to dodge it and move out of reach for a moment. I held back as I built up some magical energy ready to help me attack, but it turned out to be a mistake. With plenty of time to recover, Minsheng now came on the offensive.

Blocking what I could, I bounced around and back to try to minimize the impact of each hit. When I was sure of my move, I used magic to reinforce the strike or block but I was either exhausted from everything that day or Minsheng had upped his game because I couldn't find an opening to attack back.

You're distracted, Zephyr's voice boomed in my head, having been silent for a lot of the day.

I definitely am now, I replied, barely getting a block up in time as I danced out of attack range again.

Calm your breathing and focus only on the movement of your arms and legs. You're better than this.

Beginning to feel more than a little irritated at being told how to spar by a dragon less than nine weeks old, I tried to control my breathing anyway. I had an audience now, and to some degree they were all people who were also counting on me. I couldn't let them down, I just couldn't.

I struck out at Minsheng again. He gave me a quick flick of his fist, but then I pulled all my magic into a leg sweep and spun myself forward. He stepped out of the way, but I let the momentum carry me even farther and caught him in the side with a sharp jab. He gasped and I wondered if I'd not been controlled enough.

"Continue," he said a fraction of a second later, as if he sensed my worry for him.

Taking another deep breath while I reacted to another lunge from him, I felt for the air around me and drew on its energy.

The combination of magic and fighting was definitely getting easier as both grew instinctive. I tried to attack again, this time ducking under a punch from him, but he tilted back and kicked out slightly. I had to use both hands to block and force his foot down and away from me.

He grunted as he hit the mat harder than usual.

Better, Zephyr said.

You say that like you're some kind of expert now.

I am. Well, I've witnessed so many fights, and I remember what it feels like. Azargad's bond with Tuviel grew very strong. She taught him much.

Distracted by Zephyr's declaration that he could remember more of his ancestor's memories, I missed my next block and Minsheng's fist hit me square in the chest. It would have knocked me off my feet had I not reached back and pushed air out of my hands to jet myself back upright.

Keeping the momentum, I jabbed up. He blocked across his torso with both hands, but I had so much force it still sent him flying. Landing on a mat behind, he didn't get right back up again.

I gasped and ran to his side to help him back to his feet.

"I'm okay," Minsheng said once he was standing. "The padding took the brunt of it. But I think that's enough for one day."

With no intention of arguing, I nodded. I was more than a little tired, and it had been a long day, all of us only napping in the van for a few hours. Not to mention that I had bruises and aches from all the fighting with the agents earlier in the day.

We all made our way to the designated bed area and I was relieved to find that someone had blown my airbed up and set it in the cubicle next to my bag. We didn't have curtains, but we had sleeping bags and pillows. For now it would work. And I'd slept in far rougher situations.

"I'll put up curtains and work on some heating first thing tomorrow," Chris said to Daisy. I looked over to see her shivering, but she just gave him a small smile and said goodnight. Instantly I felt guilty. It was all my fault that they were sleeping rough in a building with no working heating in the middle of a city where an entire agency was trying to capture them or worse.

Sighing, I flung myself down on my airbed. There was nothing I could do while I was so exhausted, but I was going from the moment I woke up in the morning.

You keep sighing, Zephyr said as the dragon settled down beside the airbed and rested his head on it, right near mine.

I'm worried about the others and what I've got them into.

They're here because they want to help.

I know. But they didn't piss off an entire agency. I did. And tomorrow I'm going to do what I can to help and then I'm going to train harder than I've ever trained.

We.

I looked at him, blinking in surprise and feeling even more guilt.

We pissed off an agency, and tomorrow we're going to train harder than we've ever trained, he added.

Exhaling, I smiled, grateful for the dragon I'd bonded with. I shuffled a little closer and rested my head against his neck.

Able to hear the steady, firm rhythm of his heartbeat, I fell asleep.

CHAPTER SEVENTEEN

Standing back, I surveyed what we'd created. With a lot of help from Zephyr and the fire salamanders, the warehouse now had all the training areas we'd had in the old room. Chris, Minsheng, and I had just installed the last platform, and it all looked epic.

More than once, Chris, Daisy, or Minsheng had gone to pick up more supplies, but two days after we'd started, we'd collectively installed a system.

The area designed for me to train to fight in this building was far cruder and smaller than the last time, but the area designed for training both Zephyr's flight and mine was more elaborate, the space far larger than anything before.

"We're out of a few things we need for dinner this evening, and I want to stock up so we can lie low for a bit," Minsheng said. "Why don't you and Zephyr get familiar with everything while I head to the shops."

"I'll come with you," Chris replied as I nodded. After being in the building for over forty-eight hours I was also more than ready to leave, but I knew I couldn't, and even if I dared to try to disguise myself, Zephyr definitely couldn't be seen, and I couldn't bear the thought of being away from him even more.

It felt like I'd been cut in two when he flew above the beach too far away. I dreaded to think how wrong it would feel for one of us to be in an entirely different part of LA.

With all the construction, I'd not had a chance to train much, and I was still no closer to flying, but seeing all the different platforms, hoops and hanging ledges we'd created, I was more than eager to see if I could finally master it.

Remembering what Zephyr had suggested the first time, I started on one of the mats. I also made sure I was a good way away from anything hard or breakable in case I got this completely wrong.

Taking several deep breaths to try to calm the nerves already tensing my shoulders, I reached for the air around me. This needed to be controlled, so I took my time and tried to imagine what I wanted to attempt.

Zephyr stood nearby, acting as if he wasn't watching me but was staring instead at the younger fire salamanders as they chased each other through the maze. His head was inclined slightly more my way though, and I was pretty sure he was also a little tense.

Wish me luck, I thought, wondering if he was paying enough attention to hear me and respond.

I believe the correct human term is for you to break a leg. Although I understand this can be very painful.

It's a stupid human phrase, isn't it? I've never understood it either.

You can do this, he replied instead.

I grinned and on my next exhale I began forcing the air away from my hands and feet as well. Having started a little strong, I lifted right off the ground with a wobble, but I managed not to lose my balance as I eased off again and stabilized only a few inches off the ground. I'd achieved this much before, but I knew just hovering here would drain me quickly.

The last time I tried to move from a stationary spot I leaned forward and aimed to fly in that direction. This time I slowly increased the pressure instead, wobbling and doing my best to gently correct each overbalance as I rose in the air.

Zephyr turned his head my way, no longer hiding his interest as the fire salamanders and Daisy also gathered.

"You're flying!" she exclaimed.

The new noise distracted me just enough that I wobbled, and before I knew it I was tilting and unable to stop myself. I was about to crash headfirst into the nearest mat when I managed to bring my arms around fast enough to slow my fall and carefully righted myself again.

Daisy came around to stand in front rather than yelling from behind, and I smiled at her.

"Sorry," she said.

"No worries. Going to have more than that going on the next time we run into the agents. I need to be able to handle a distraction or two and not lose my cool."

Daisy relaxed at my words, clearly relieved that she hadn't done anything wrong. Already feeling tired from all the magic use, I slowly lowered myself to the ground again. As soon as my feet were firmly planted I grinned. It might have been fairly short and uneventful, but I'd had my first successful flight.

You wait until you can really fly about. Zephyr stepped closer, stretching his wings. I got the distinct impression that he was asking me to fly with him if I could. For the first time I wondered if he got lonely in the air. Or even just lonely in general. He was a dragon, and possibly the last of his kind.

I'll try again once I've had something to eat. Controlling all this air makes me hungry.

Bring me some of whatever you get.

I rolled my eyes at Zephyr's request. The dragon seemed to always be hungry, especially as he was still growing. Getting enough food in for him was going to become a mission all of its own at some point, I didn't doubt.

After grabbing a snack for both me and Zephyr, and having a moment's rest, I went back to the mats. Once again, I reached for the air around me and channeled it where I wanted, lifting myself upwards slowly again.

I didn't feel quite so tense, finally able to fly in at least a basic fashion. As I lifted a little higher, I tried to inch forward. This time I was a little steadier, but as soon as I started trying to move I grew less balanced.

Despite the extra wobbles and adjustments I needed to keep making, I managed to propel myself forward. With my body aching, muscles I'd possibly never used protesting at the strain, I was considering landing again and calling it a day when Zephyr leaped into the air, flapping his powerful wings nearby.

Again, I wobbled, the air his wing beats stirred up

adding to the difficulty, but he moved off ahead of me and then hovered, each downbeat of his wings like a rhythmic pulse.

I fixed my eyes on him instead of the ground and moved closer. At first I took it slowly, but my grin grew wider as I closed the gap. When I was only a little way away from him his mouth fell open in what appeared to be a scaly mimic of a smile.

Having expected him to stay there until I reached him, I was then surprised when his wings propelled him higher again, carrying him up above my head, while our gazes remained locked.

Pushing myself even harder, I rose, trying to follow. At first it went well, but as I drew close again, the next downbeat of Zephyr's wings sent me off-balance. I reeled backward and couldn't seem to correct for the sudden movement. Spinning a couple of times, I found Zephyr suddenly close, his paws catching me and helping me stop spinning.

No matter how hard I tried, however, I couldn't get myself flying again, and we landed on the mat, my body lying under his. For a moment, I barely dared to move.

I could see why dragons scared people. Despite being young and fairly small, Zephyr towered above me, the scaly ridges on his face and the horns and ridges down his back making him look like a fearsome beast.

He jumped to the side so I could get myself up and then tilted his head back and studied me again, the two of us standing very close.

I don't think it will be long before I can carry your weight into battle. Zephyr seemed to smile at this too.

While that would be epic, I want to make sure that if I fall, I can catch myself as well. It frees you up to attack whatever or whomever might have knocked me from your back.

An important option. Zephyr puffed up his chest.

Chuckling, I tried to look more serious. I wasn't sure I managed it, but Zephyr didn't appear to be bothered by my humor. Instead he flew upwards again.

Trying again? he asked. I considered it, but as I went to make my arms rigid by my sides and bear my weight, they started to shake right away, and nothing I did would stop it from happening while I got off the ground.

"Do you know when Minsheng and Chris left?" Daisy asked a moment later, breaking the sort of stalemate I was having with myself.

"A while ago," I replied, a little vague while I thought about a more accurate answer. "They probably ought to be back soon."

Daisy frowned and made her way to the warehouse back door, the entrance we'd decided to keep using despite me now having keys to the main doors. The less used this building looked the better.

I followed, trying to remember exactly when they'd left. Now Daisy had drawn attention to it, I couldn't be sure how long they'd been gone and if we needed to worry or not. Both of us stopped by the back door, listening.

"It's no good," she said. "I'm too worried about them. I'm going to have to at least see if the van is where we leave it or not. I'll be back in a few minutes."

My voice didn't seem to work so I simply nodded and waited by the open door.

Do you want me to go up to the roof and see if I can see them too? Zephyr walked up as well.

I shook my head, partly because I didn't want to be by the door without backup and partly because I couldn't bear the idea of him being that far from me. I also wasn't sure if he'd be able to see anything more than Daisy was going to.

Every second I waited by the door for Daisy to come back felt like a minute and every minute like an hour. By the time Daisy had been gone for four minutes I was peeking down the alley, and another couple of minutes later I was imagining every possible reason why both Daisy and before that Chris and Minsheng might not make it back.

The thoughts ranged from the less serious alien abduction to the more obvious and simple reasons like traffic, with a thousand in between. In short, anything could have happened and I was determined to torture myself with every single possibility I could think of.

Relief was instant when Daisy came back around the corner. She had a massive packet of toilet paper under one arm and bags of shopping in the other.

I exhaled, all the pent-up tension leaving me, but she didn't look happy, and when Minsheng and Chris came around the corner after her, both of them were hurt. They still carried bags between them, but Minsheng was sporting a bandage on one arm and was clearly struggling with what he carried in that hand. Chris had a fresh large bruise on his head.

Throwing caution to the wind, I rushed down the alley to help with the bags.

"What happened?" I asked as I took the bag Minsheng

was carrying with his injured arm and then lifted one of the two Chris carried in the nearest hand.

"Once we're inside," Minsheng replied, before going back to gritting his teeth.

As soon as we had it all on the warehouse floor, Daisy locked the door.

"I'll start putting this away," she said, looking pointedly at Chris. He nodded and followed her silently with the bags. The salamanders rushed over and Zephyr said something to them. A moment later they were picking up whatever they could and scurrying up the stairs with it.

It didn't take long for the food to all have disappeared and for it to be just me, Minsheng and Zephyr left in the warehouse.

"Who hurt you?" I asked, although I already suspected the answer.

"Agents. They're all over the city looking for you. Didn't recognize us at first and we thought we'd got away with it, but then another arrived outside the grocery store and they started shooting."

I put my hand to my mouth, fearing he meant real bullets.

"Tranquilizer darts," he clarified, possibly picking up on my distress.

I nodded and sighed. That was something. I dreaded to think what it would feel like to fight the agents if they'd been using real bullets the whole time. There was quite a good chance we'd be dead by now.

"We got in a bit of a close-quarters argument as we tried to get our shopping out of the store," he said. "And of course, we didn't want them to see the van."

"Did they?"

"I don't think so," Minsheng replied. "We knocked them out, but as you can see, it cost us to have to defend ourselves like that."

"I expected the agents to be patrolling the places where we've been before, like the beach. Not hanging around grocery stores," I said, frustration welling up inside me.

"We were sloppy too, but it changes our situation, Aella. We need food. And they are now well aware we're still in the city and are planning on sticking around. Even if they know nothing else of our whereabouts, they can keep the pressure up, and there's far more of them then there is of us."

I nodded and sighed. While a part of me didn't want to hear it, Minsheng was right about everything he'd said.

"I'm going to have to tell the organization I'm injured. And I think Chris may have already prepared his injury report as well."

"And they're bound to demand we go to the Sanctuary again."

"Of course. They think we'll be safer there. They believe you and Zephyr could benefit from it." Minsheng looked at me, his eyes gentle and an almost pitying smile on his face. I exhaled loudly, and put some distance between us as well as breaking eye contact.

"What do you want?" I asked.

"I want you safe, and I want you to have the opportunity to learn more about yourself, as always."

"Running from these agents is not something I think I can do. Not now. I have a building. A place to actually call my own." I stepped back a bit, feeling anger rise inside me.

185

How dare the agents try to take my life from me again? I didn't want to hurt anyone, and never had, unless it was self-defense.

But that wasn't all. There were too many unknowns. We also couldn't be sure that if we ran from the city, the agents wouldn't just attempt to track us elsewhere, and I pointed out as much.

"We can't be sure, but the pattern they follow is usually predictable enough. And the Sanctuary is not only better hidden than this but you can learn more there."

"I understand, but we're not leaving yet," I said, the words coming out in an angry rush, my fists clenched. "If we're running low on food and can't get any in LA we'll run, but until then we'll stay and do our best to beat the agents back."

I stormed off before Minsheng could respond in any way. I wasn't leaving. I'd just made this place feel like home, and begun training again. I couldn't lose a valuable building someone had been protecting for me.

CHAPTER EIGHTEEN

I landed on the mat as Minsheng broke into a broad grin and Daisy started clapping. I'd just flown around the building. It was several days after the agents had accosted Minsheng and Chris while buying us groceries and I'd had my first flight, but I'd made steady progress each day since. Today I felt like I'd properly flown.

My flying skills were now good enough that I could mostly move where I wanted as long as I didn't want to get there too fast or fly for too long.

Since the attack, I started each day listening to any interesting information the transceiver bug I'd planted in the agents HQ picked up on, and then I trained and trained. The others often helped, but there was only so much they could do. Each day I grew a little stronger, and each day I felt a little more ready to face the agency.

Thankfully, we'd not had any more run-ins with them, although Chris was the only one of us who had left the building since he and Minsheng had been attacked buying groceries.

As soon as I flopped down after my flight, Daisy handed me a granola bar and a bottle of water. I gobbled down the first one before gulping on the latter.

"I can't wait to see how the agents react when you fly at them," Daisy said.

As I pictured how Knox might respond, I couldn't help but grin. Our next battle was going to be more than a little interesting.

"What's next?" she asked as Zephyr came closer and sat down too.

"I need to fly faster," I replied.

"I meant after you'd learned to fly." Daisy put her energy bar wrapper in her bottle and screwed the lid back on. She then rolled it across the ground. Newton and two of his siblings darted out of a gap between the mats and the wall and chased it.

While we watched the salamanders play I thought about it. I didn't actually have a clue. I'd been so focused on flying and so much had happened since then I wasn't even entirely sure what I could do.

While we'd been snacking, Minsheng had gone up the stairs to do something else, so I left Daisy with the salamanders and went to find him. Zephyr followed, as he often did. I was grateful for his presence beside me. Thoughts of the agents and the battle we'd have to face sometime soon made me nervous. I had been unlucky recently and exposed others to far more risk than they ever should have faced at other times.

I found Minsheng sitting on the small sofa Chris had picked up for us that morning before he'd had to go do a job somewhere. In his hands was one of his books, but I couldn't see which one until I got closer. It was one about the old tribes of each race, something I found hard to imagine. If there was just me left of the elven race, then where had all the others gone?

"Looking up anything in particular?" I asked, not sure where else to begin the conversation but knowing I needed to if we were going to keep making progress.

"Seeing if the tribes hold any clues to where a sanctuary of some kind might be. Or how we'd find it," Minsheng replied, before sighing. "I'm not getting very far."

I frowned, annoyed that he was still pulling in that direction when I'd already said I wanted to stay.

"The organization has insisted I do so," Minsheng added, making it clear he'd read my facial expression. "And it's prudent to be prepared for all eventualities."

I opened my mouth to rant, but instead Zephyr nudged me toward the sofa and I sat down. He then sat as well, resting his head on the arm of the sofa near me.

"Why don't you tell me about them? Maybe I can help," I said without thinking.

"We don't know much about the original tribes. They lived before humanity really flourished, although they were still around for some time after that."

"How many different tribes were there? Just one for each race, or many?"

"There were a few. The dwarves have three settlements mentioned, all of them near mountains," Minsheng replied, flicking to the dwarven section of the book he was reading. There were several old-looking maps, one of them clearly of the Rockies. "I think this is where my ancestors are from, but I've not been matched to any particular line."

I couldn't quite tell but it sounded like Minsheng was sad about not having an epic ancestor, so I leaned in a little closer to see the book and whispered, "I'm sure whoever you're descended from was a phenomenal dwarf."

"Maybe one day we'll find out. But they weren't the only race who liked those areas. Gnomes lived in many different ones across the world. They were probably the most spread out. They looked just like halflings, and many tribes intermingled with the humans so much that there were very few pure gnome lines left. I think any descendants are like Chris, mostly human."

"They'd struggle to hide among humanity otherwise."

"Possibly, but there are abilities that the races have between them, which make it easier than you'd think."

"So it's not just the elves who can do magic?" I asked.

"Sort of. Only the elves can control the elements the way you do. The dwarves have great skills with crafting, especially metalwork. They could enchant all sorts of items. Probably where your necklace came from."

I reached for the necklace without thinking, the charm always slightly warm to the touch.

"What about the gnomes?" I asked.

"What could they do?" Minsheng replied. I gave him an affirmative. "The gnomes have probably one of the more varied sets of magic. But it's also more subtle. They were often skilled with potion-making, but not just basic alchemy; they had a refined element about it."

Minsheng paused for a moment, and I thought he was finished, but he flicked to a different page of the book and scanned a small section of it before carrying on.

"Apparently gnomes are also capable of manipulating

the senses. A powerful gnome can create all sorts of different enchantments. There's a mention of shields made from nothing but air, although the elven section mentions that too, and even concealment spells. They can trick you into thinking you're drinking the finest champagne when all you've got is muddy water. They can make you smell smoke from a fire even when there isn't one."

"Cool," I replied, imagining how much fun that could be when playing pranks on people.

"It's one of the reasons the Sanctuary is probably so hard to find."

"Because they've got a gnome who can help them conceal themselves," I finished for him.

"Highly likely. I wouldn't be surprised if they're also nomadic."

"So why aren't elves, dwarves and gnomes around so much anymore?" I asked a moment later.

"I think the answer to that is complicated. Humanity has a habit of trying to destroy that which it doesn't understand. All that which is too different. And elves, dwarves and gnomes are very different.

"The races warred with each other for many, many years. Eventually elves, dwarves, and gnomes managed to find a sort of truce but they were too outnumbered by humans to ever have a safe place on this earth. Instead of worrying further and taking even more innocent lives, most of them decided to hide or to leave."

"You said leave before, but go where?"

"I'm not entirely sure. The old law books refer to several places that some of these races must have come from in the first place, but whether these are another dimension, or another planet in space, is not understood for sure."

"I'd like to find more elves like me someday," I said.

"I'm sure we shall. I'd also like to find more dwarves." As Minsheng spoke we both looked at each other, and an understanding passed between us. Neither of us felt quite like we belonged in the current world as it was. To find others like us would make us feel less different and less unwelcome.

"Anyway," Minsheng said. "There doesn't seem to be anything useful in this book. You should get back to your training, and I will see what else I can find."

Minsheng got up and took the book he was holding back to the small bookshelf Chris had made him. I half-expected him to pull a different one off and begin looking through that too, but he didn't, instead going down the far set of stairs toward the reception area and kitchen.

Although a part of me wondered if I should follow him and check he was okay, it was clear he'd just shut the conversation down. I decided to give him space and headed back to the main warehouse.

I wish I could remember more of what Tuviel and Azargad experienced, Zephyr's deep voice said in my head, sounding a little sad.

Do you think it would help?

Perhaps. I think they would have known of the Sanctuary.

Assuming it existed when they were alive.

The times weren't peaceful. They went on the run as much as us, but humanity was no kinder to them.

That sucks.

A little, but they shared a strong bond, like us, and also like us, they had good friends. Zephyr sounded wistful, almost as if he was lost in a memory.

Can you remember everything Azargad experienced?

Not everything, and it's not like I suddenly know I have all these memories. The majority of them seem to be from experiences of dragons at a similar age and not just Azargad. But I don't get a new memory and know I've got it. I'd be doing something, listening to you and Minsheng talk, or even flying, and a memory would come to me as if what's happening now has reminded me of my own memories.

That sounds like it's both helpful, so you don't get overwhelmed as new memories are unlocked, but also unhelpful. That you might not realize you know something.

Pretty much. I do know I'm looking forward to spending as much of my life as possible with you. Some of the dragons I remember didn't bond with an elf in the way you and I have bonded and Tuviel and Azargad did. Some of them merely lived as dragons, mated with other dragons and then died.

I stopped walking, still at the foot of the stairs of the warehouse, and turned to face Zephyr. I could only begin to imagine what it must be like to have these memories of so many ancestors in your head, and to feel the associated emotions that went with those memories. But I did know the bond between us was growing and I was just as grateful to have him by my side.

Not sure what else to do to show him that I felt similarly, I reached forward and hugged him as best I could.

A strange *pop* sound drew our attention to the far corner of the warehouse. By the time we looked, Daisy was standing there with one of the agents' dart guns in her hand, aiming it at the target a hundred feet or so in front of her on the furthest end of the building.

Lifting my eyebrows I went over to her, wondering what it was she was trying to do.

As I walked up, Zephyr coming with me, she opened up the dart gun and fished out some of the ammo. It wasn't the same darts we'd been using on the agents and they'd been using on us. But the shape of them was similar although not uniform.

"Have you been making more ammo?" I asked.

Daisy laughed and shook her head.

"Not exactly. These are a form of training ammo. I managed to get some second-hand from a shooting range that was shutting down. Think of them like the rubber bullets the police use for riot control."

"Are they effective in fights?" I asked, having never been hit by rubber bullets.

"They can be, but that wasn't what I was using them for. I wanted ammo for target practice, and for all of us to practice. If we're going up against the agency again, then those of us who don't have funky superpowers need to be able to help."

I nodded, a strange lump in my throat as I thought back to what Zephyr had just said. I did have good friends.

For a moment, I watched as Daisy refilled the gun with a slightly different size of ammo and shot at the target again. This time she seemed to be satisfied, shooting the entire magazine. As she finished, my jaw fell open. Her scores on the target were impressive.

"I had no idea you could shoot so well," I said. "Will you teach me?"

"That's the plan."

"Daisy here used to sneak off to the shooting range when she thought no one was watching." Chris grinned as he came out of the small maze we had set up, carrying his toolbox. He'd probably just installed something else inside, a surprise for the next time I ran through it.

"I didn't sneak off. No one asked where I was going, so I didn't tell them. Besides, Minsheng had his thing. He's always been a good teacher, and he's been doing martial arts for as long as I can remember. When the organization decided to pay him to do research as well, I knew our lives could get interesting. And then you showed up with your gadgets, gizmos and your funky magic tricks and I knew I'd better get started on learning something that might help in the future."

"Well, it sounds like you succeeded," I said, looking again at her score on the target. "I don't know many people who can shoot that well."

"I had a good teacher," she said, her familiar grin creeping across her face. "Now, come on. Let's see how well you manage."

Without waiting for me to reply, she handed me a gun. I stood at the mark she'd made on the floor, and I took a deep breath. As I exhaled I lifted the gun and aimed as best I could. Not breathing for a moment, I shot as many darts as were in the gun.

"Pretty good for a first attempt," she said as she fetched my target as well.

"I had some practice shooting agents," I explained.

"Well it's gotten you off to a good start." She fetched me

a new target and handed me more ammo. "But I'm sure we can all do better."

With Chris taking an interest too and putting down his toolbox, there were soon three targets on the wall and all three of us lined up.

Daisy was by far the best shooter, but with each target and each round, I got a little better. Chris started poorly, his hands shaking more than ours, but even he improved over the course of the hour or so we practiced.

When Minsheng appeared to let us know he had fixed us some dinner, Daisy offered him a gun as well.

"No, it's a waste of target and darts at this point. I can shoot well enough at a large target like an agent, but I'm by no means a marksman."

"You'll never get better if you don't practice," Daisy argued, giving her brother a disapproving look.

"No, but all my life, I've had the luxury of doing the things I'm good at. Learning new things is always hard, and let's face it, you're far better at it than me."

"I had to be better than you at something. At least it's something useful."

The two of them chuckled as they wandered back toward the stairs.

Chris put his gun down as well, clearly having had enough of the target practice. But I let them go without me for a moment. I knew my abilities had helped defend me from bullets and darts from the agents in the past. And I'd begun to wonder if they could help me shoot even more accurately.

Curious, I reloaded my gun and put up a fresh target. However, instead of just shooting, I used my abilities to create a small funnel of air directly from the end of the gun to the center of the target. This time, as I shot, more of the darts hit the center of the target.

It was my best attempt yet. Without the others there to see, I compared it to Daisy's best. My score wasn't quite as good, one or two of my darts still going too far out, but it had definitely made a difference.

You know, Zephyr's voice appeared in my head, *you could do that with my breath weapon too.*

What do you mean? I asked.

You could use your ability to direct it at agents. Turn it into a projectile.

That's not a bad idea. Did you just think of it?

I've just remembered it.

He didn't need to say any more. I placed a hand on his shoulder, letting him know I was there for him. We'd figure this all out together.

CHAPTER NINETEEN

Panting hard, I came to a stop at the exit of the training maze, Zephyr landing beside me a moment later. As I did, Daisy clicked the timer.

"Twelve minutes and nineteen seconds," she said with a grin on her face. I held my thumbs up, still not able to speak.

That's our fastest, Zephyr said in my head, not even slightly out of breath despite having flown through it far faster than ever before while taking out the targets along the way with me.

I sat down and grabbed the nearby bottle of water as I nodded. We'd been in the warehouse for over a week now, and I'd trained almost every spare minute. But I still wasn't sure if we could best the agency again. Not yet.

Chris had managed to simulate more of their new tech, the shields, net launchers and the gas masks they used to protect themselves from Zephyr and my abilities, but it wasn't quite the same as facing a real situation.

Each day I trained I also grew stronger, my body able to

handle more of the running, jumping, and even the slow flying I could do now. My ability to control the air was also growing more natural, quicker and more intuitive. It felt like it drained me less. I knew both of these things would lead to me being more effective in battle.

Still, I didn't feel ready. Not to face so many more agents who weren't just being told to overpower me but genuinely wanted to. Were almost desperate to in Knox's case.

As my breathing eased, I got to my feet again and looked over the maze. There were still a couple of sections I could improve on the current layout. Then I'd ask Chris to make it harder.

"We're low on food," Minsheng said as he and Chris appeared.

I frowned and stared at him. The last time he'd gone for food he'd been hurt, and the agents had almost caught him. The last thing I wanted was for him to put himself in danger again. But what other option was there if we needed food?

"Chris and I have discussed how to do it best," Minsheng continued. "We've waited until dark and we're going to go to a store farther away."

Despite the extra care to be safe, I still didn't like it.

"Is there another way we could get food?" I asked.

Minsheng shook his head.

"If we do anything that involves ordering online we create a way for the agents to find us," Chris said. "This way they might find Minsheng and me, but they never find you or Zephyr."

I opened my mouth to object further, but Minsheng put a hand on my shoulder.

"I know you want us all to keep safe and wait until you're ready to take on the agency. And you've been training incredibly hard to ensure you can soon, but we need to get in some food before you're going to be ready. It's a quiet Tuesday evening. It's the safest it's going to get."

Letting out a sigh, I nodded. He was right. I already knew I couldn't attack the agency yet, and that meant now and then someone had to risk getting us food. If Chris and Minsheng were taking every precaution to keep safe, I couldn't exactly say no.

"Come back as soon as you can," I said as they headed toward the door.

"Of course. We've got a list and it should be pretty quiet. Chris also has a couple of charms that will mask us a little."

I raised my eyebrows as Daisy turned to the part-gnome techie.

"Charms now too, bucko? When did you learn to charm stuff?"

"I didn't. They're a little something I borrowed from a friend when I told him that we were in a bit of a bind. You know my gnome blood isn't strong enough for me to create magic charms."

"Pity," Daisy said. "I'd have loved one that masked the smell you all leave in the toilets."

I chuckled as I watched them go. Daisy just looked at me and shrugged, smiling at her own words.

Despite the humor and their confidence, I felt a strange weight settle into the pit of my stomach, and it didn't go away. Chalking it up to worry and anxiety about their safety while they were out of the warehouse, I went back to the start of the maze along with Zephyr.

Still growing at an alarming rate, Zephyr's head now wasn't much below mine, although his body still only came up to my waist.

Ready? I asked him.

He let out a roar and launched himself into the air, although he didn't lift up much higher than me. Unlike the first maze Minsheng had created for me in his training room, this one was far higher and had several areas closed off like the ceilings in a building. This was entirely to mimic the offices the agency was in, but it also served to help teach Zephyr how to fly in enclosed spaces.

"Go," Daisy called from somewhere I couldn't see.

Instantly I sprinted forward, pulling the training gun from the pocket in my pants. As I turned the first corner, I brought it up and fired at the first target as it swung up from the floor. It carried a projectile weapon of its own, but I hit it before it could fire, and the wiring Chris had included was clever enough to stop it from firing its weapon.

It flopped back to the floor and I jogged over it and then took the next right. Zephyr flew above and just behind while we were in the maze normally, but the next target was his, and he darted forward as it swung out near the top of the construction. He turned and raised one wing a little to bring his front claws to bear. Slamming into the target, Zephyr stopped it from dropping debris on me or my path through.

Grinning at the dragon's flying skills, I ran on. Our next

target wasn't one we directly had to go past, but if we didn't take it out Daisy would add several seconds to our result. Heading past an open doorway on the left, I twisted my body sideways and shot through it. At the same time, Zephyr turned his head and exhaled one of his paralyzing gas clouds into the room.

Moving on with the target neutralized, we wove back and forth inside the maze, only heading to dead ends and into rooms if there were targets we needed to shoot, hit or gas. For the most part Zephyr stayed in the air, but occasionally he landed to help me with an area with more ground obstructions and targets.

I was almost at the end, hurrying around yet another corner, when I fired wide. My dart caught something more important and ricocheted. Zephyr dove, but that put him in my way, and the target we hadn't neutralized also shot a device like a taser. Getting hit with it docked us another couple of seconds.

As I tried to roll out from under Zephyr and give him the space to get out of my way, the taser got me in the arm. It was set to low, but it still stung and made me drop my gun.

Zephyr bit down on the target and almost broke it, triggering the retraction as he pulled back.

As I pushed to my feet, I grabbed the gun and glanced at the target. My dragon's teeth marks were all over the top section. Chris wasn't going to be pleased, but I was more concerned about them getting back from the grocery store okay.

You're distracted. Zephyr's voice was calm, not sounding like a reprimand so much as a statement of fact.

I'm worried about our friends.

Me too. Next time we should go, even if we hide in the van.

I began to form an objection to the words, wanting to keep him safe in the warehouse too, but as we finished off the last part of the maze and rushed toward the exit where Daisy would be waiting, I knew I liked the idea. That way if anything did happen, we'd be close by and could intervene.

"What took you so long?" Daisy asked as we emerged and Zephyr landed. She stopped the clock, but her gaze never left me, clearly expecting an answer. I didn't give her one at first, too out of breath.

"I missed a target, and got hit," I said, choosing not to say why. She didn't need me to add to her worries. Minsheng was her brother, and it was clear she cared deeply about him.

"That's your slowest time today," Daisy replied.

I nodded, pretty sure that meant it was time to call it a day.

"If you don't need me anymore, I think I'm going to go find the fire salamanders and chill out for a bit," Daisy said, heading to the far end of the warehouse and the stairs up to the living area of the building. At this time of day, the salamanders would either still be on the roof, or if it was colder, they'd have come back in and curled up in the blanketed warm area Chris had made for them to sleep in.

I didn't doubt that if I followed I'd find Daisy on the roof with them or tucked in her own bedroom area, the curtain drawn across to make it clear she wanted to be alone.

Sighing, I leaned toward Zephyr and stroked his shiny bronze scales. He tilted his head so I could scratch behind his ears and then let out a noise partway between a purr and a growl.

Why don't I get us both a snack and you can tell me about any new memories you can think of that you like? I suggested, something that was becoming more frequent between us. Using my ability definitely made me hungrier than normal, and Zephyr's appetite continued to grow along with his size, so I knew he'd say yes to the offer of food. And since he'd told me he didn't always know when a memory had unlocked unless something reminded him of it, I'd been asking him to tell me more about what he did remember.

Only if I can have the leftovers from dinner, he eventually replied.

Did you leave any at dinner?

Zephyr snorted and shuffled his wings as if he was indignant about my question so I rolled my eyes and started walking. We both knew there were leftovers. Minsheng and Daisy always cooked far too much knowing Zephyr, the fire salamanders, or I would eat it over the next few hours.

It wasn't long before the two of us were sitting in the small dining area we'd created beside the kitchen, tucking into reheated leftovers.

So what was Earth like when Tuviel and Azargad lived? I asked Zephyr, keeping the words in my head.

Nothing like it is now. It was centuries ago, perhaps even millennia. It's hard to tell exactly how many years. I don't have every single memory from every single one of my ancestors. Just from the moment that each offspring was born.

Zephyr's words made sense. And I couldn't believe I

hadn't even thought about that yet. It must be so confusing for him.

Azargad was a great dragon, but many feared him. When Tuviel was with him people were more kind, but it wasn't the same as it is now. Or the many years in between when so many of my ancestors basically hid themselves.

What's the most recent thing you remember?

My mother, I think. She lived in a mountain range but I don't know where yet. I just have these images of these great white snowy peaks. She met my father there. I don't have any of his memories, but I remember the two of them meeting. That's my most recent memory.

I didn't know what to say to that. It sounded like a very important memory and I wasn't sure how much I should pry. We'd also finished eating, and I was beginning to worry about Minsheng and Chris again.

Why don't we go and sit under the stars while we wait for Minsheng and Chris to come back? Zephyr asked.

Once again I found myself wondering if Zephyr could hear more than just the thoughts I tried to project. If he could, he didn't let me in on the secret. Instead of asking him, I nodded.

Although there were a few clouds in the sky, there were more than enough clear patches where we could see the stars. I exhaled, instantly feeling a little less tense. There was something about nighttime and the night sky. And it was even more moving for me when the moon was out.

Some people spoke of finding their happy place in nature. Some type of environment that calmed them, at the beach, or a forest. I found mine looking up at the stars at night.

As Zephyr sat down beside me, he rested his head on my shoulder and I leaned his way as well. It seemed I wasn't the only one who liked nothing more than to sit and look up at the little lights in the sky.

We were still sitting that way when Chris and Minsheng pulled the van up a block down the road. From our perch on the roof we could just about see them, and I broke my contact with Zephyr to go down to the back door and help them bring the food in.

Relief flooded through me when I found them completely unharmed and Minsheng assured me that their trip had been entirely uneventful. Even Chris grinned as he handed me a bag full of groceries.

No sooner had Zephyr and I carried the first load up to the living area than all the salamanders rushed to help.

Before I could stop them, the younger ones rushed out of the back door after Minsheng and Chris as they went to get another load from the van. I rolled my eyes, but I couldn't help but smile as I listened to their excited chatter. They didn't like being shut up in a warehouse for a long time either.

Given how late it was, and how Minsheng and Chris would have to make fewer trips with all the extra help, I didn't think any more of it.

Even Daisy made a reappearance, helping me and Zephyr shuffle everything from the door up to the living area and into the fridges and freezers. But as we went back to the door for the fourth time, none of the others had come back yet.

"Stay here," Daisy said as she walked down the alley.

Before she could get to the end, the others reappeared, carrying the last of the food between them.

I smiled, relieved once more. It was so easy to get worried when things took just a fraction more time than normal.

But Minsheng didn't look happy as he followed everyone in. Before I could ask what was wrong, he ushered everyone to take the last of the food to the kitchen. It didn't take long for us to get everything put away, but before anyone could leave, Minsheng put something down on the dining room table, and beckoned us over.

"The young fire salamanders just found this on the bottom of the van." Minsheng looked at Chris, and the part-gnome's face got a lot more serious.

"Is that why you took so long the last time you went out to the van?" Daisy asked.

Minsheng nodded. "The salamanders kept making a fuss underneath the van, and when I bent down to find out what they were up to, Newton and one of the others were pulling this off the bottom."

As I came closer, I inspected the small item. It was round and had something sticky on one side. On the other was what looked like the tiniest aerial and a blinking red light.

"That doesn't look like anything good," Daisy said, her words matching my thoughts.

"It's not," Chris replied. "It's a tracker, and there's only one group of people that would be tracking us."

My blood ran cold as I realized what that meant. Minsheng and Chris had accidentally led the agents right to us.

CHAPTER TWENTY

For a moment no one said anything. All of us thought we'd be safe here for a while. At least long enough to grow stronger, to train and to take on the agency on our own terms. But it looked like we weren't going to get that luxury.

"We should pack up what we can, whatever will fit in the van along with us, and leave," Minsheng said.

"No way," I replied. "We don't even know if they're coming straight here."

"Do we even know for sure it's them?" Daisy asked.

"Who else would want to track us?" Chris asked. "I'm convinced it's the agency. But we'll have a window before they attack. They'll wait for a little while to confirm that the tracker is stationary here. Then they'll need to gather the full force of the agency. There's no doubt they'll use every single agent they have this time."

"Yes, if we give them time to, they'll come here with every single agent they have." I folded my hands across my chest. "We must attack them first."

"No," Minsheng replied. "We aren't ready."

"I don't think you ever think we're ready, brother," Daisy said.

Minsheng opened his mouth to respond but Chris put a hand on his shoulder and Minsheng calmed.

"I think if we attack the agency," Daisy said, now looking at me, "we'll be walking into a sort of trap. The second we attack, they'll call in every agent they have anyway. But instead of being somewhere we're familiar with that we've prepared to aid us, we'll be in a place that benefits them. Let's make this warehouse the most danger-ous, unsafe and hostile environment for those agents that we can. We've got warning. Let's use it."

As Daisy spoke her eyes lit up, and I could see Chris nodding along as if her words were persuading him as well.

Ignoring all of them for a moment, I turned to Zephyr. He was the most vulnerable, even more vulnerable than I was. I wanted to know what he thought.

My memories are full of my ancestors hiding and running. Except for Azargad and Tuviel. I don't want to run, but if I'm going to fight, I want to do so in the smartest way possible. Zephyr came closer as he spoke, his violet eyes staring into mine.

You want to defend the warehouse?

I'd like us to defend the warehouse. Together with our friends, I think we can do it.

I sighed, realizing the others were also staring at me. Was this my decision? Should this be my decision? I didn't know, but it was clear they were waiting for me to tell them my thoughts.

I didn't answer right away. The idea of sitting around waiting for someone to turn up was not fun, but what Daisy had said about taking the fight to the agency was true. It was their territory, their ground, and although we'd won there once, there were a lot more of them now.

I knew I didn't want to run away either, but Minsheng was just trying to protect us. Running away now was the only way to be sure that all of us would survive and not be captured. But I knew if we started running now, Agent Knox was the kind of person who would keep pursuing us. We'd either have to find the Sanctuary before he did or leave the country for good.

"We'll defend the warehouse," I said, looking at every one of them in turn.

I expected them to ask questions, or to complain. Maybe even argue back but none of them did. It was as if a decision was all they really needed.

"I can reprogram the targets inside the maze, and make them attack the agents instead. Between them, they're almost a little army of their own," Chris said, grinning.

"We can move the maze," Minsheng added. "Attach it to the door so that they have to come through it."

At this Daisy grinned, beginning to chuckle to herself at the very idea of it. Even I smiled, imagining the different targets dropping their weights, shooting the tasers and otherwise generally making a nuisance of themselves.

"We'll need to barricade the main entrance, make it impossible to get in that way." I looked around at the things we could use to prop up against the doors and make them even harder to get through.

"I think I can make some kind of gas bomb, if Zephyr will breathe into a few things for me," Daisy said.

"I can help with that too," Chris replied.

This seemed to finish the discussion as Chris and Daisy went back through the warehouse to begin making preparations.

Minsheng only hesitated a moment, before he got the fire salamanders to help him move items of furniture and block off the main doors.

Not sure how to help, or even where to begin, I used my powers to help push along the furniture and save some of their energy.

"There, that should stop them getting in this way, but if we really do need to flee, you should be able to move it out the way quickly and get us out and toward the van." Minsheng went to head up the stairs to go to the main section of the warehouse and join the others, but I held up my hand for a moment and stopped him.

"I don't understand why you're not still trying to persuade us to leave. Some of us could get hurt." As the words came tumbling out, I realized I was terrified of the others getting hurt or anything worse happening to them.

Minsheng stopped and looked straight at me.

"I also don't understand," I added, "why everyone looked at me to make the decision."

"Because you're our leader. You're the one with the abilities, you're the one who descended from Tuviel, and you're the one who bested the agents the first time. You've become a leader whether you intended to or not."

"But none of you even asked me to justify myself.

You're just trusting me. What if one of you gets hurt? It'll be my fault."

"Yes, and no. You can't control the actions of the agency and they're the ones trying to hurt us. But the weight of this decision does rest on your shoulders. The very fact that you're worrying about the safety of your friends and the people you're making the decision for shows that you're not making this decision lightly. Now it's down to all of us to do our best to keep all of us safe. When the time comes, you'll need to decide if we should run away or not. Can you do that?"

I bit my lip, not sure if I could. I was about to open my mouth to say no when Zephyr came close again.

I have a memory of one of the first times Tuviel led Azargad and others into battle, as well. She shook with anxiety and nerves. Didn't know she was ready. Azargad didn't know if he was ready. And we are never going to entirely know if we are ready or not.

Then maybe this is a good thing. Maybe we were spending too much time here trying to make ourselves feel ready for something we'd never feel ready for.

That is what I believe.

Zephyr's words brought me some comfort. I turned back to Minsheng and lifted my head.

"If the time comes that we need to run, I will make sure everyone knows. And I'll make sure we get out okay."

"Then we can ask for nothing more," Minsheng said, his eyes lighting up as he looked at me. "And I'll be proud of you no matter what happens in the next few hours."

I nodded, feeling tears sting the back of my eyes and

worry settle like a brick into my stomach. His words had been honest, but they'd also given me confidence.

They won't take us, Zephyr said as we ascended the steps up to the main living area.

No, but I won't leave anything to chance. If you think of anything we can do to give ourselves an advantage, let me know.

Of course. But know there's already plenty we can do. The agents are going to be walking into a trap and they will think they're ambushing us.

As Zephyr finished speaking I felt a little lighter. And satisfied. Giving Agent Knox a taste of his own medicine from the ambush at the restaurant would make my day.

While Minsheng, the salamanders, and Zephyr and I had been barricading the front entrance to the building, Chris and Daisy had been busy in the warehouse. The targets and shooting range were gone, all the weapons and empty containers sitting in a pile. The targets inside the maze were also no longer in there, Chris walking out with one as we appeared.

Zephyr started filling the containers Daisy had with gas while the rest of us continued to dismantle the maze and move it to the door. Instead of making a maze with dead ends and hidden targets, we constructed the longest labyrinth we could, targets in the places most likely to hamper the agents' movements. We wanted them exhausted before they could get anywhere near us.

It wasn't easy, pulling apart the panels and moving them, all of them heavy enough to need two people and the roof only easily removed by Zephyr as he flew. We were still only halfway through when I noticed it was past midnight. I stopped for a moment, my arms aching and my body weary.

A moment later Daisy yawned at me, the weapons she'd made us as ready as they could be. Her yawn was instantly contagious and I replicated it before Minsheng and then Chris did the same.

As one, we all took a break while Daisy made us some caffeine-rich drinks and I considered how we'd handle the agents once they'd made their way through the labyrinth.

Dotted around the higher section of the warehouse were even more platforms, some of them suspended on chains and others attached to the walls. I knew, without a doubt, that I wanted Zephyr and me up above the warehouse floor, but it was also a safer place for some of the others if we could get them up there more easily.

"Don't even think about asking me to hide up on the platforms," Minsheng said as he looked between me and the area of the warehouse I'd been focusing on. "I hate heights, and I don't think anyone should be up there who can't get back down in a hurry."

I nodded. I'd been having similar thoughts, but I'd not been sure. If he thought it was best to only have those who were capable of getting back down quickly up there, then I wasn't going to argue.

"I'm good with a rope," Chris said. "Attach a rope to that platform over by the top of the stairs. If we need to beat a retreat I can shimmy down and we can run out the back."

The salamanders can run up and down ropes too. Zephyr's voice appeared in my head. I looked his way to see him conversing with the fire salamanders, the matriarch of the salamander family letting out little roars and chitters to explain something to Zephyr.

More rope it was, then. Despite my tiredness, I went to fetch some. We didn't know how long we had, and I wasn't going to have anyone vulnerable and on the ground still when the agents got here. I felt pretty confident that Zephyr and I would be okay, but we could both fly. As long as we didn't get hit by too many tranq darts, we'd be fine.

As soon as I brought the rope back out, Zephyr flew up to the platform above the stairs with one end of the rope. I then used my powers to head up along with him, trying not to think about how all my previous flying had been over areas that had mats underneath in case I got it wrong. This time I was starting from the small landing at the top of the steps and I could easily fall on an array of metal weaponry sticking up all over the place.

As I concentrated on heading toward Zephyr, I kept my ascent true and made it to the platform. While everyone else went through the maze, I attached ropes to all the platforms, running them in a web the salamanders immediately made use of.

Watching them run back and forth across all the platforms, playing a game of chase while they couldn't do much else to aid us, made me wonder what the warehouse would look like when this battle was over. With any luck, the agents would realize there was no beating us and I could negotiate a new truce.

But every time I thought of Agent Knox and how he'd sounded in the few conversations I'd listened in to, I felt that hope die. Would he truly leave us alone? Or was I going to need to do something more permanent?

I didn't know if I could bring myself to kill anyone, but I had a feeling I was going to find out at some point. After all, humanity was clearly scared of what mythical creatures could do.

As I landed again, Daisy came over to me with some of the weapons and ammo.

"Put this wherever you want it for the battle. And Chris asked if you or Zephyr could dump his stuff on the platform for him so all he has to do is climb up on it," Daisy said as she handed me two sets.

I nodded, not sure exactly how I'd get them up there, but willing to try. I was less help with moving the maze and everything else they were doing to prepare.

Tucking my pistol into one pocket, and the ammo into the pocket on the other side, I felt fairly balanced, but that still left me with everything for Chris, which included some of the strange gas grenades Daisy had made from Zephyr's breath.

Use a bag, Zephyr said as he came over. *Any kind. Then I can carry them up.*

I need the flying practice. But a bag is a good idea.

Zephyr dipped his head, his way of nodding, and then flew up anyway. Almost as if he was working out where he would want to be to begin our defense of the warehouse, he landed on the platforms one at a time and looked around himself. Leaving him to it, I found a small bag I could put on my back and concentrated.

It was getting easier to automatically find the right amount of pressure to lift off the ground in a careful, controlled way, but I was more heavily laden than normal, and at first nothing happened.

Pushing a little harder, I finally rose off my feet and into the air. I wobbled more than normal, my balance different now that there were objects in my pockets and a bag on my back.

Thankfully, no one was watching as I shakily made my way up to the platform. As I got close and looked up, something somewhere went wrong and I overbalanced. Tilting forward, I panicked and reached for the nearest rope as I deactivated my powers. I managed to get my hand on it, but I slid slightly, the friction making my palm burn with heat.

Dangling from the rope more feet above the ground than I liked to be, I got my breath. Holding onto the rope with both hands, I slowly pushed some more air out of my feet to make myself lighter as I went up the rest of the way.

It wasn't the perfect way to have gotten there, but eventually I was on the platform. I pulled off the bag and put it down in the center of the platform, making sure none of it would roll away if any of the suspended wood wobbled a little. With that done, I made my way to the edge of the platform and faced the next one. It was the one I'd chosen to sit on for battle, out over the warehouse but low enough I was going to be able to shoot easily.

This time I wasn't quite so unbalanced, and as I pushed off the platform with my powers and moved forward I managed to make my way without needing any ropes.

It wobbled as I landed on it, almost overbalancing. A quick forward jet from one of my hands helped me right myself. And then I was standing on a platform out above the warehouse, able to survey everything we'd laid out for the agents.

I unloaded my pockets and simply stopped and stared for a moment. In just a few short hours we'd turned the warehouse into an obstacle course the agents were going to have trouble getting through. And even when they came out the other side, they were going to come face to face with us. Feeling a little more hopeful that we had a chance to win this thing, I flew myself back down again.

As I landed, Chris, Minsheng and Daisy came out of the maze, tools in hand, faces stern, and a similar gleam in all their eyes. They were as ready as I was.

"I'll take watch on the roof," I said. "Why don't all of you get some rest before they arrive."

"I don't know if I'll be able to sleep much but it's worth a try." Chris patted me on the shoulder as he wandered past. Daisy didn't say anything as she followed, leaving me with Minsheng and Zephyr.

"I'll relieve you in a few hours if they haven't shown up already," Minsheng said.

I considered arguing, but I knew if they were going to take that long, some sleep would be appreciated.

As everyone else went to settle down, I made my way up to the roof. I'd expected Zephyr to go with them and try to sleep as well, but he came up to the roof with me. As I found a place I could sit while still keeping an eye on the surrounding roads, Zephyr came and sat beside me. I leaned into him as he leaned into me, his body warm against my back.

We are going to make them regret hunting us, Zephyr said. *We're going to show them that mythicals are back and we're not afraid anymore.*

CHAPTER TWENTY-ONE

I lost track of time, sitting on the roof with Zephyr. I only got up once, to fetch the transceiver and listen in to the agency. With any luck, I'd get an even earlier warning from that.

But it was as quiet as the warehouse was. Everyone around me slept, including Zephyr.

Alone with my thoughts, I was only growing more nervous and anxious about the upcoming battle. More than once I'd almost got up and woken the others, deciding that it would be better for us to run away and come back when we were stronger. But every time I was about to get up I would think of Agent Knox and how determined he would be. I didn't doubt he would simply follow us.

Knowing this warehouse was mine also gave me a strange sense of ownership. I may not have decided to own it, and I hadn't purchased it myself, but for some reason it was mine and I wanted to defend it.

On top of that, I wanted to defend my friends. The fire salamanders had done nothing but want to exist, much the same as Zephyr. It wasn't fair that the agency wanted to take them away just because they'd been born. I couldn't let that happen.

Eventually, Zephyr woke again. I reached out and stroked his head, running my hands down his smooth scales.

Still waiting? he asked, his voice soft and deep in my head.

Still waiting.

Is it possible the tracker wasn't theirs?

I've considered that, but I'm not sure who else would have put it there. The only other shadowy entity is whoever bought this for me. And they already know where I am.

Then I wonder what they're waiting for.

Me too... And I'm not enjoying the wait.

Before Zephyr and I could say anything else, there was a sound behind us and Minsheng appeared, coming up from the warehouse below. He yawned while he carried two mugs of coffee.

I reached out for one as he sat beside me.

"Not going to persuade me to try to sleep, then? I asked.

"I figured you wouldn't want to. I barely slept anyway. Not exactly easy when you know some vicious people are about to attack you." Minsheng smiled at me.

"Tell me about it," I replied, sipping the hot beverage and enjoying both the taste and the warmth as it spread through me.

"Have you heard anything?" Minsheng asked as he pointed at the transceiver. I shook my head.

"I wondered if maybe they realized the bug was there." The words slipped out, betraying my fears.

"I doubt it. It's easy to think of what ifs in a situation like this. The truth is probably something logical. They're waiting for more agents to be awake, or they're being extra careful about making sure the tracker is stationary here. All sorts of reasons why they might not have attacked yet but will still be coming."

It made sense, and I appreciated Minsheng's calm. I didn't know how he managed it but he was always so chilled out. Almost as if he'd seen it all before.

"Have you done anything else while you were waiting for me?" I asked. "Did you just run restaurants in Chinatown?"

"I've done many things, and all of them have served one purpose or another. But mostly I went where the organization sent me."

"How did you start working for the organization?"

"They reached out to me. I don't know how, but they seem to know things. They can be secretive, but I believe they're just trying to protect mythicals and the other races. So they only tell you what they need you to know."

Minsheng paused, and I waited for him to continue, his gaze off ahead, like he was remembering something.

"They told me to wait in LA many years ago, that they thought an elf was coming, an elf who would bond with a dragon. They asked me to make sure she was prepared and that she did find her dragon. And then you turned up in my restaurant. And you had your dragon and you'd already proven yourself to be incredibly resourceful."

"You said you'd noticed me earlier in the day. Why didn't you come help me then?"

"Because I wasn't sure it was you. I'd been waiting for

so many years. I was expecting someone who would be using their powers and would know how to do all sorts of things. In short, I let my assumptions get in the way." Minsheng sounded sad as he spoke, as if he couldn't forgive himself for what he'd done. But I'd still managed to find him, and he'd still saved me.

"I'm sorry I didn't trust you right away," I replied. "I should never have left your restaurant after that first meal."

"You had no idea who I was. And I hadn't been prepared for my ward to show up not even knowing what a Shishou was."

"Well, I'm glad you waited so long. I hope I don't let you down."

"You could never let me down. You're already so much more amazing than I could ever have hoped. And you've taught me all sorts of things already."

Before Minsheng could tell me what those things were the transceiver started crackling, picking up on the sound of an opening and closing door. Footsteps and the squeak of a chair followed.

I turned the transceiver up, bringing it closer so Minsheng could listen as well. It sounded like something was finally happening.

"You'd better have called me in here at this ungodly time of the day for a good reason, Knox," Agent Crawley said.

"I found her. Her and everyone else." The triumph in Knox's voice was clear. I wanted to punch him in the face.

"How? Where?"

"One of our agents managed to sneak a tracker on the van they were using. We've been keeping an eye out for it for over a week. Since we've seen them at the grocery store." Knox paused, having confirmed our suspicions.

"May I remind you that day at the grocery store was yet another muck-up I had to clean up."

"That, it may have been. You haven't been without your own need for cleanup operations. But sometimes a little mess is worth the end result."

"So far you don't have any results."

"But I'm about to. The tracker led to a warehouse not too far from Chinatown. And only a few blocks from Aella-Faye's original apartment. We suspect it might even be where she found the dragon egg in the first place."

"Go on," Agent Crawley replied, not sounding angry for the first time in the whole conversation.

"I was wary at first. Trackers can stop in strange places, for various reasons, but I had someone check it out. Someone who didn't look like an agent. The van has stopped, and the rest of them are in a warehouse not too far away."

"Did you see them going in and out of the warehouse?"

"No, but we don't need to. When my undercover agent came back and said where the van was, I had a look at the area. The warehouse isn't on the map. Not only that, when I tried to find out who owns that bit of land and what it was actually used for, I found several dead ends. The kind of dead ends that you get when people are covering something up."

"What kind of cover-up?"

"I'm not sure, but when I did finally find out what was there and who owned it, I found it was an abandoned warehouse, set as unsafe for humans to enter, and you'll never believe whose name it was in."

"Spit it out, Knox," Crawley demanded.

"Aella-Faye. It's in her name. But that isn't even where the mystery ends. It's been in her name her whole life."

There was nothing but the sound of the chair creaking again, and I almost swore. Whoever it was who had put the warehouse in my name had helped lead them right to us.

"Then you have permission to go and retrieve them. But I want them alive and well enough to talk. I want to know who's helping them. Jacobs will want to know who's helping them."

"*I* want to know," Knox replied. "Don't worry, we won't use lethal force on any of them."

"Good. You can use the entire agency and any other resources we have available. But Knox, you'd better get it right this time, and I want the minimal scene possible. You go in, you capture them, and you bring them out."

"Understood. My men are ready. I just need yours."

"Go. Be back here by dawn with good news."

A moment later, the door opened and closed again. I exhaled, having barely been breathing while they spoke. They were on their way now. It was only a matter of time.

"I'll go let the others know that they are on their way. And then check that everything is ready. Why don't you stay here until the first agents arrive and then come down and let us know?" Minsheng asked as he got up.

I handed him my empty coffee mug and nodded. Watching him go, I felt a familiar tension in my shoulders and a knot in my stomach. It was definitely easier to feel confident while Minsheng was nearby.

We should block off the roof when we go down, Zephyr said. For a moment I blinked, surprised that we'd forgotten this entrance. It didn't seem like a way in when you thought about normal routes, but who knew what tricks the agency would use?

I think we should get one of the fire salamanders to watch it, in case they break through, I replied, my eyes on the roads ahead of us. *We don't want to get cut off, or attacked from behind.*

I'll go tell them now, and then I'm going to go fill up that maze with gas.

I grinned as Zephyr got up, shook and stretched his wings, and padded toward the door. My amusement was short lived, however. I couldn't help but be aware of this third person Knox and Crawley had referred to twice now. Who was Jacobs, and how much of a problem would he be?

It made sense that there wouldn't just be one agency building in only one city, but how interlinked were they? If I beat Knox and Crawley, would I just have to face another agency, and another, until there were none left? Was that even possible?

With no way to know, I could only wait. Despite Knox having left Crawley's office several minutes ago and his declaration that his own men were ready, the minutes continued to tick by, leaving me with my thoughts and fears. This was probably our last chance to run and hide before they came, but I couldn't bring myself to get up and offer that option to the others again.

Tired and feeling it, I sat and watched. Every car that appeared made me tense, until I could tell that it wasn't a black sedan and it bore no threat. I relaxed again, but not as much as before, until I was wound as tight as a coil. Somewhere below, I could feel Zephyr moving around, and I hated the distance between us. It added to my unease.

There were still a few hours of night left, but whatever happened, Crawley and Knox wanted it over by dawn. By then, we'd either be captured, or I'd have sent the people trying to make mythicals disappear a very obvious message.

Come on, Knox. Let's get this over with. I want to know which one of us is right.

But still time ticked by, and still I waited. Whatever Knox was doing, he was going to turn up prepared. I could only hope we were equally so.

This had to work. Or I'd doomed us all.

CHAPTER TWENTY-TWO

Finally I spotted the telltale signs of agents. One, and then more of the black sedans they all drove. They were followed by a set of larger black vans.

The moment the vans pulled up outside the warehouse, agent after agent poured out, all of them carrying guns and shields already.

I quickly retreated, grateful none of them had spotted me.

They're here, I told Zephyr, hoping he could pass it on to the others for me before I even got down to their level.

At the same time I hurried through the roof door and used my powers and some brute strength to push a set of empty filing cabinets we'd found across it. Hopefully it would keep anyone trying to come that way from getting through until we'd had a chance to deal with the others.

We can tell. They're already trying to get in the main entrance, Zephyr replied a moment later. I spotted one of the salamanders tucked up in a corner near the top of the stairs down to the living area of the warehouse where I'd found Zephyr. He was on top of the stair railing, and I didn't doubt he could turn and scurry down it incredibly fast if he needed to.

And the back? I asked Zephyr a moment later. I could hear the banging by the front door now and I peeked down the stairs that way. Another of the younger salamanders was on the steps, also watching. It was the best we could do to cover those two entrances.

No sign yet, but they're going to get a nasty shock when they do.

I grinned, thinking of the maze, but as I appeared on the landing in the warehouse I noticed things weren't the way I'd left them anymore. Zephyr stood on the ground, exhaling thick clouds of gas into the labyrinth.

Chris was on the platform above me, and Daisy and Minsheng were both behind tables on the floor, using them like shields and waiting with guns in hand. All the other equipment we had was in different places, martial arts weapons were now gone entirely, and I had no idea where. The dojo mats had been piled up smack bang in the middle of the warehouse. All of the salamanders sat on these, a rope running down to them from a platform overhead.

Finally, all of the books and other tech was up on this secondary floor, tucked in our bags along with what looked like basic belongings for all of us.

I frowned when I saw the bags, but I wasn't going to bring it up. If we needed to flee, we needed to flee. It would be important not to leave anything that mattered behind. If I hadn't been so determined to stay, I knew I'd have felt grateful, but I wasn't going to complain.

Instead, I nodded to Minsheng and Daisy. It was clear

they knew we had trouble on the way.

"Any idea how many?" Minsheng asked as I waited, not going up to the platform yet.

"No," I replied, "but at least thirty at a guess."

"Hells' bells," I heard Chris say from above.

I took a deep breath, my heart already faster than normal and my stomach now so tense it was one hard knot. Only once I'd tried to calm myself did I attempt to fly again.

Lifting up, I looked toward my goal. The platform where I'd left my gun. I was only partway there when I heard a bang and the rush of feet as they tried to come inside. It was followed by swearing.

At first I managed to keep flying and stay focused, but another loud bang as one of Chris' traps went off and an agent yelped in pain made me wobble. I grabbed a nearby rope and steadied myself, this time remembering to keep my powers active, and then I flew.

There were more yells and more than a few swear words. I couldn't help but grin, feeling safe on my platform above the chaos.

After one last long exhale, Zephyr withdrew from the edge of the maze and flew up to another platform.

Stay safe when they come through, I said to him. *They'll aim for you more than the others.*

And you, he replied.

I sighed and nodded, not doubting Zephyr was right. The agents were going to be trying to get us the most, but they had to get through our labyrinth first. And they had four people and an assortment of mythicals waiting for them on the other side.

There were more yelps and the sounds of clattering inside the trapped maze. A couple of times the whole construction shook, some of the panels bending under the force of either the agents or something they carried, but as yet none of it gave. White vapor escaped here and there, and it was slowly drifting out of the edge of the maze toward Daisy and Minsheng, but as it got closer to them I sent a very gentle breeze to blow it back inside again.

If waiting on the roof had felt tense, this was a thousand times worse. I knew the agents were there, and doing their best to get to me, but I didn't know when the first would emerge.

Slowly the labyrinth went quieter, and I could hear more banging toward the main entrance to the warehouse. I glanced that way, but I had to resist the temptation to fly back to the living area and check no one was coming. Had we made it so difficult for the agents to get in through the back entrance and maze that they were willing to keep bashing through the other route? I had no idea.

As a salamander appeared and let out a little screech, I had my answer. I pushed off the platform without thinking, still clutching my gun in hand.

Flying far faster than I ever had before, I hurtled toward the small landing as Zephyr flew that way too.

Minsheng glanced my way as I landed a little ungracefully, his eyes asking me to be careful while his mouth didn't dare make so much noise. I nodded, and ran to the top of the stairs.

The second I rounded the corner I spotted the problem. The agents had managed to push the top corner of the main door open, splintering the wood slightly. When we'd stacked up furniture in the way, it hadn't got that high, but now that they had that bit open, they'd stuffed some kind of rod through the gap and were pushing it in. No doubt when they applied pressure to the other end it would help push the obstruction out of their way. I couldn't let it happen.

Zephyr must have had the same thought as I. He flew and landed on top of a wardrobe before exhaling through the gap.

I heard agents swear as I half-ran and half-propelled myself down the stairs. The gap was higher than I could see through from there, so I also pushed myself upwards with a couple of air blasts and landed on the top of our furniture for a moment. No sooner had I done so than a dart came through the gap, barely missing Zephyr as he pulled back.

Blasting air out the gap for a moment, I leaned forward and aimed my gun out. There were several agents, all of them holding shields, but none of them wearing gas masks. One was on the floor, as rigid as Zephyr's victims usually were. The agents shot at me the second they saw me, but I kept up the steady stream of air and let them waste some tranq darts.

There wasn't much of the agents showing through the gap, especially with the shields they carried, but I aimed as best I could anyway.

I let off three rapid shots, hitting two of the agents although one was close to a miss, the dart almost scraping the agent's arm rather than fully hitting. It was enough, however, and both agents collapsed.

Can you push that pole back out? I asked Zephyr. *I'll keep the agents busy.*

Should be able to.

Zephyr leaped into the air again and came down on the pole with his front paws before a down flap of his wings caught him and stopped him from falling off it. The force was enough to push it out. I got down and pushed the furniture back into place with my air and body. It shut the entrance again except for that small gap.

As Zephyr threw himself down against it to hold it shut, I looked for something bigger and heavier to block that section. The only thing I could think of were the weights from the small gym Minsheng had put together, but I wasn't sure where he'd moved them.

Stay here, I told Zephyr.

As you wish, but I have no desire to be a glorified door wedge for long.

Noted.

Hurrying up the stairs again, I looked around. In the back of one of the cubicles where the few bits of gym equipment Minsheng had acquired. I grabbed the weights I could carry with my hands, and used the air around me to lift the rest, and then hurried back to the main entrance with them.

Move, I said as I floated the weights already in the air closer. As Zephyr flew off the pile, I replaced him with the heavy objects, floating all of them up one by one until there was a tall pile on top of the wardrobe.

The wardrobe seemed to sag a little, but it couldn't be helped. Hopefully it would hold. If nothing else, it helped weigh down the obstruction and made it even harder to shift.

For a moment I listened as the agents continued to try to get in that way, but eventually it went silent, the wardrobe and weights still holding.

I think we can head back now.

I agree. Zephyr made a few noises that the tiny fire salamander responded to, and then we hurried back up the stairs.

Still only halfway up, the other little watch salamander of ours came into view, squeaking and squawking from above.

I sprinted up the last few stairs, heading straight for the roof, Zephyr only a fraction behind me. There wasn't room for him to fly above my head in the enclosed space so he was forced to land and bring up the rear.

As I turned the last corner, only four more steps before the roof door, I ground to a halt. The agents here had pushed all the furniture aside, getting the door partway open, and were now using a sort of lever in much the same way the agents by the main entrance had.

I blasted outward with my air and knocked the agent holding the pole off his feet.

Another tried to replace him and brace himself with a shield, but I swept sideways with the air on the roof and sent him sprawling onto the shield to one side. Then I swept his body backward as two more agents came sprinting at me. The agent I'd sent flying knocked one of them off his feet, but the other managed to jump over him.

Zephyr bounded forward, exhaling into the jet of air I was creating. The guy was blasted with the gas. He held his breath for a moment, still coming forward and reaching for a gas mask he'd had dangling from his belt.

I hurried toward the pole along with Zephyr, and together we pushed it out. Not letting go of it just yet, I swung it, catching the only agent of the four currently standing. He inhaled in pain, and I blasted more of the vapor cloud Zephyr had created into his face. It wasn't perfectly effective, my blast dissipating as much vapor as it moved, but in this close a proximity, it was enough.

Within seconds he was paralyzed in an almost fetal position.

More gas, I told Zephyr as the other agents started to get to their feet, their intention clearly to attack.

Zephyr roared as he exhaled again, and I did my best to control the white mist and send it to the agents. One of them was already fixing his mask in place, but the other two hadn't been prepared. As I actively tried to steer it around their heads, the two were paralyzed, just enough getting into their lungs.

As the final agent got to his feet once more, striding toward me and the pole, and pulling a gun, Zephyr took to the air again, taking the agent's attention off me. Before he could shield himself adequately again, I pushed so much air at him so fast that he stayed upright, and pretty much flew backward so hard and fast he fell off the roof.

I rushed forward, horrified to think I might have killed someone, but as I went to the edge I saw he was still attached to some kind of rope that the agents had fixed to the side of the building and no doubt rappelled up.

Before he could pull himself back up, Zephyr bit the rope and snapped it. This time he really would have plummeted to his death, but I made a cushion of air underneath and set him down gently.

More agents came running up, sending three more ropes and attachments onto the side of the building. As Zephyr stomped and bit at the pulley systems, I used the air to pull all three of the agents on the roof toward me, hurl them over the edge, and then drop them on the agents trying to climb up.

As the agents got back to their feet, they started shooting. I did my best to send the darts off-course as Zephyr smashed more of their equipment. We then backed up away from the edge to see if they'd try to shoot up more grapples.

They didn't, and instead I heard more of them running down from the alley, clearly deciding that was the best route in despite the labyrinth of paralyzing gas and traps.

We should get back to the others, Zephyr's voice sounded in my head, but I was already turning to do just that. Just in case, I planned to seal the doors back up as well as I could.

On the way back inside, I took the pole they'd been trying to prize the door open with and stuck it through the handles on the inside, wedging it in the gap.

Then I moved the filing cabinets back in place as well. Now both of the other entrances were more secure than they had been. Once more I left the young fire salamander to keep a lookout on the banister rail.

As I went past, I stroked his head.

"Good job," I said, but I didn't linger. All the agents would now be focusing on one way in only. And that meant, despite the obstacles, Daisy, Minsheng and Chris were about to be overwhelmed.

CHAPTER TWENTY-THREE

Arriving back in the main area of the warehouse, I once again tried to fly over to my platform. So focused on the coming agents that I barely thought about it, I actually flew more accurately. I landed on the platform only a fraction of a second after Zephyr alighted on his.

The agents were still trying to navigate the labyrinth, and the gas had continued to spill out of the exit. Despite having used my powers enough during this battle to already make myself feel tired, I created as gentle a breeze as I could to try to blow the gas backward into it and keep the vapor away from Minsheng and Daisy.

It mostly worked, although a few wispy tendrils were spread around or torn up. I could only hope it wasn't enough to knock any of us out.

Minsheng glanced up at me, and I gave him another nod before I reloaded my gun and got everything else ready. Already I'd taken out some of the agents and I didn't doubt our labyrinth had probably neutralized a few more.

But any moment now we were going to have to face the rest.

There was another yell, followed by a second, this time a lot closer to us. A moment after that I heard Chris chuckling and found myself wondering which of his obstacles had just been triggered.

I didn't know how long we'd been defending the warehouse already, but once again time seemed to slow, all of us waiting for the agents to emerge. I had a moment to calm, to recover and to reflect. The initial nerves I'd felt at the beginning of the battle had disappeared while I'd actually been in action and pushing back agents trying to breach our defenses.

Now, however, they returned with full force. With the other two entrances now so well shut off every single agent would be coming at us through here, it put the others at a greater risk.

My worries were soon replaced by the need to act. The first sight of movement at the exit to the maze had every one of us shift slightly and aim our weapons.

An agent emerged from the maze, carrying his shield and creeping forward slowly, and it sounded like he was talking underneath the gas mask he wore. Behind him came another agent, also wearing a mask.

They spotted Daisy and Minsheng first, and shot at the pair. Daisy shot back, but her dart bounced off the shields. Instinctively I raised my gun to shoot over the top from the angle I had, but I stopped myself at the last minute, and instead blasted both agents with a powerful gust of air from behind.

Their shields were wrenched from their grasps as both let out curses.

Daisy and Minsheng shot one of them each, and both went down on top of their shields.

The next two agents to appear were more wary, no doubt realizing their comrades were already unconscious. They tried to hold their shields across the labyrinth exit and shoot over them. Daisy and Minsheng dived for cover and I hesitated, unable to pull at their shields with a gust of wind without also pulling the gas out of the maze and into the warehouse.

Before my eyes, the two large salamanders got down off the mats and scurried to the labyrinth walls. Escaping the agent's notice, they then slid through gaps in the formation. Next thing I knew, there were yelps and pained cries, and a moment later the salamanders came scurrying back out again. Both agents collapsed backward, their shields falling on top of them.

What's just happened? I asked Zephyr. I knew the salamanders could spit acid if they really wanted to, but that didn't knock agents out.

The salamanders bit the agents, drew blood, and the gas could get into their system enough to paralyze them.

But the salamanders...

Held their breath.

Neat, I replied, remembering how the gas had begun to have an effect on me the one time I'd been exposed to it wearing a gas mask. Eventually it was absorbed through the skin. It sounded like a break in the skin made it even worse.

While I didn't particularly want to kill the agents coming after me, I had no problem with one of us hurting them. Not when so much was at stake. And I wasn't going to stop the fire salamander family from acting as they saw fit. The agents had stolen one of their babies and injured the poor thing. If I'd been its mother, I'd have a lot of rage and wish for payback.

I heard the sound of dragging, and the agents' feet disappeared into the fog. This only made me grin. They would expend energy getting their own men out of the way and be exposed to the gas even longer.

Admittedly, it wasn't ideal for all of the agents to be paralyzed. Compared to the tranquilizers, it wore off quicker, and an injury or broken equipment that meant they couldn't attack again at all would have been better.

The last thing we wanted was for the odds to turn after we'd been battling for ages because the agents who had been paralyzed at the beginning could now move and fight again. It might be the difference between winning or losing the battle.

The next set of agents soon appeared, however, distracting me from my on-the-fly strategy thoughts. Coming farther forward this time and not wasting their ammo, they looked around them although they were hunkered down behind their shields. They tried to form a barrier farther out, but I wasn't going to allow that. One again, I pulled at the shields, gusting them, but the agents stood more firm and fought against my powers.

As one wobbled slightly, I noticed they'd modified the insides, now strapping them to their own wrists so their grip didn't fail in the same way, and padding the internal structure so it also helped funnel the air to the sides rather than acting like a sail I could blow over.

Growling, I shot one of the middle agents, catching him on the top of the shoulder from my platform above. The moment he collapsed it broke the shield wall and the two on either side were off-balance, one trying to catch him. Minsheng took the opportunity I'd given him and shot some more as well. Rubber bullets pelted the exposed agents, grunts of pain accompanying every hit.

No sooner had the three remaining agents passed their fallen comrade backward and another agent had tried to shuffle forward than I shot again. This time I went for the newcomer as he walked. He continued his momentum forward as the sedative took hold, and fell into the agent in the middle of the new shield wall.

At the same time I added a blast of air to it, knocking all three agents onto their fronts. Daisy, Minsheng and Chris opened fire, hitting the agents with darts and rubber bullets until they were either bloodied and retreating in a hurry, or unconscious on the floor.

We didn't get a reprieve, however, as this time several ran forward, shooting as they did in several different directions. I had to tuck behind my platform for a moment, darts hitting the suspended wood from underneath.

As the men and women came forward, even more appeared, these ones aiming more exclusively for Minsheng and Daisy, Chris still hidden from view. They weren't firing darts either, their own ammunition switched over to the more painful rubber bullets.

Anger filled me and I blasted all of them with as much

air and force as I could muster, coming in from the sides and front. It knocked the two outer agents off their feet, sending them down, but it brought more of the fire my way.

I was quick to notice that for the most part they fired darts at me and rubber bullets at the others. Somehow I had to make it clear I wasn't okay with that. A moment later I noticed all the rubber bullets on the floor. They might be useless to the agents attacking but they weren't for me.

Shifting to the other side of my platform, where I could see the piles of rubber bullets on the floor in front of the tables shielding Minsheng and Daisy, but the agents couldn't see me, I focused on taking control of as much air as possible. I lifted the rubber bullets, and flung them as hard as I could at the agents.

Despite hurling them semi-blind, I could hear the effect, and I scooted back to the other side to see three more agents down and even some damage to the maze walls.

Picking up some bullets again, I hurled them into the maze, hearing grunts of pain. I grinned at evening the odds again temporarily as the warehouse went silent.

Again, I lifted what bullets I could and held them in the air in a small cluster above the labyrinth exit, waiting. Still, no one came out.

A moment later there was loud bang and panels to both the left and right gave out, agents coming out of both new exits. I redirected the ammo I held, hitting one of the squads in the side. A dart whizzed by my head and another hit my platform as I pulled back.

I glanced back to see Chris finally entering the fray

with more force, throwing something at the agents in the other group.

There was a loud bang and the agents were knocked off their feet. The few behind who managed to stay upright seemed to have gone blind or deaf. I wasn't completely sure which. They were no longer fighting and were trying to head back into the fog-filled maze.

By the time I'd noted that, however, more agents were pouring out of the other new hole and the original exit. Now everyone joined the fray, Zephyr darting off his platform and the salamanders running toward the maze as well. I switched from offense to defense, blocking darts and bullets and jetting blasts of air at agents' guns to try to keep the other mythicals safe while they attacked.

Shots rang out, and despite my best efforts, Zephyr took a dart to the underbelly. Not before he knocked two agents off their feet, however, and kicked another in the head, knocking him unconscious.

The fire salamanders bit any agents close enough to the gas for it to knock them out, or spat acid and became little balls of fire that hurled themselves at any agents farther out.

The fires caught on all sorts of things, from parts of the maze to the agents' clothing and weapons.

Shouts filled the air, and a part of me felt momentarily sorry for our attackers. Burns hurt. And fire could kill. But then I remembered what they were here to do. Could I blame the salamanders for defending themselves with the only natural weapon they had? Not at all.

I renewed my attack, driving the agents and the fires back toward the labyrinth. The flames spread, and pretty soon the entire wall on this side was one big flame, and smoke was rising to the roof. A sprinkler system came on, but it was old, the pressure was crap, and with all the platforms, it barely did anything to slow the fire.

It did mean I was getting wet, however, one of the sprinklers almost directly above me.

For a moment the agents pulled back and the fire salamanders did the same, returning to the pile of dojo mats in the middle of the warehouse. I used my powers to direct the flow of water to where it was needed most. Managing to put out some of the fire and dampen enough of the maze, I halted the spread for now.

The calm I needed to do so was shattered, however as the agents broke through more maze panels, spilling out to the right hand side. Daisy and Minsheng didn't have a direct line of fire, the mats in the way, but both moved to the mat pile. The salamanders rushed forward again, and I had to kneel to get line of sight.

Once again, I pulled guns in all sorts of directions, but mostly upwards, trying to stop the agents shooting my friends. Zephyr took to the air again, flying over and dropping things on the agents' heads.

I hadn't realized what he carried, but I soon recognized some more of the grenades Chris had. They went off, and again confusion reigned.

The agents didn't stop coming, however. Zephyr's gas had clearly dissipated in the maze in the sections from where they were pouring out. I focused on the arriving agents, using air to yank at their guns and pull them out of their hands if I could. It made their shots go wide even if I didn't succeed in wrestling the gun from their grasps.

Any guns I did get, I pulled back toward us, dropping them in a pile behind Minsheng and Daisy. More agents went down as Daisy took every advantage she could in the chaos to hit the agents with darts, but Minsheng was soon hit with one as well, and a rubber bullet smacked into Zephyr a moment later.

With the fire salamanders attacking, Zephyr couldn't breathe more gas, and I had to be much more careful with my attacks. Also, as I pulled away more guns, the agents resorted to hand-to-hand combat.

A few of them tried to charge Minsheng and Daisy, using their shields to get close and then barreling into the two defenders. I growled, trying to yank away the shields as well, but I wasn't always fast enough.

As even more agents appeared and one of the salamanders was hit by a dart, the fire it bore going out as it was sedated, the salamanders either side reacted, grabbed it between them, and the whole family scurried back to the mats.

In the small reprieve this bought the agents, they regrouped, coming back into a shielded huddle and firing out. I blasted them with air, but tiredness hit me like a brick wall. I'd overdone using my powers and didn't have much left in the tank.

Get the salamanders to fall back, I told Zephyr, but as the agents shot at them, they panicked. They became balls of fire again, setting the pile of mats alight.

Daisy and Minsheng were forced to retreat to their original positions, and even I could feel the heat as the plastic coating of the mats melted and the stuffing inside caught and went up in flames.

The stink was awful, and the smoke rose in dark plumes. Still the sprinklers tried to combat the fires, and they'd succeeded in some areas, but the mats were just too flammable, any water that had fallen on them previously having slid down and off the plastic so they weren't really wet. And with the presence of the fire salamanders in the middle, still balls of fire, it made it even harder for the sprinklers to put it out.

"Fall back," I yelled, knowing the ones of us on platforms would soon struggle to breathe. As Zephyr and the others hurried back to the landing, Chris hurled two more of the strange grenades from his position.

A fraction of a second after they went off, I blasted off the platform, fear and desperation making me go faster than I usually would. I almost collided with Chris as I landed on the landing at the top of the stairs. Crouching, I turned and used the last of my energy to blast thick gray smoke down on the agents and block their view so Daisy and Minsheng could climb the stairs without being shot at.

As Zephyr landed, and he, Chris, Minsheng and Daisy retreated to the doorway behind, I looked for the fire salamanders.

I could just about see them in the middle of the fire, safe from the agents for now. It wasn't a perfect or long-term safe place for them to hide, but I had a feeling that this battle wasn't going to last much longer.

CHAPTER TWENTY-FOUR

As I exhausted the last of my powers, my body almost sagged under my own weight where before I'd felt strong and full of adrenaline. It was as if the life had been sucked out of me in one big pull.

Without my ability holding the thick smoke away and over the agents, it quickly billowed up and toward us. I stumbled back through the door, finding Minsheng as he reached out to steady me.

A moment later, he pressed an energy bar into my hand.

"It'll help while we hold them off," Minsheng said.

I nodded, trying not to think about what was happening behind me as I devoured the bar in a few quick mouthfuls I barely chewed. I could hear gunshots by the time I was done. Turning, I pulled my dart gun and hoped I could make the last few shots I had count. Maybe after that, I'd be able to use my powers again.

The agents might have been getting closer to us and driving us back, but we'd taken out a large number of them, and I saw Daisy hit two more before the return fire drove her behind the doorway again.

The next time she stuck her head out to take a shot, I went with her, but an agent had managed to get higher in the air, using a rope to get to one of our platforms. He shot at both of us with a quick precision that resulted in both of us feeling the sharp sting of a dart.

Daisy pulled back, already passing out, but my elven abilities fought the sedative, more used to the chemical the tranquilizers were laced with. It left me with a clear enough head that I shot back at the exposed agent, hitting him twice to be sure.

As I pulled back, he crumpled, unconscious. I saw him fall, then heard a thud and what sounded like a cry. He must have landed on top of another agent.

While the sedative rushed through my tired body, I could only sit and try to fight off the sleepiness. Chris chucked some more flash bombs, causing more chaos and making my ears ring, and then Zephyr came forward and exhaled his gas out of the doorway while Minsheng picked up Daisy.

Once again, we retreated as I heard the clatter of agents on the stairs. I just about managed to get my legs under me and bring along my dart gun, and then Minsheng was pulling me down behind the sofa.

Zephyr didn't come with us, flying instead to the opposite end of the room, no doubt intending for us to form a double-edged attack. I tried to focus and bit my lip when I saw the tip of a gun come through the door.

The second I saw an agent I fired, taking him out, and the next one as well. But more came, and as I tried to shoot the third, my gun clicked to let me know I was out of ammo. No more darts.

Minsheng took over as I fought to keep myself awake and clear-headed. I was pretty sure they'd upped the dose from the first time they'd shot me with the tranks, and I wasn't sure how I was managing to fight the sedative off, but it didn't seem like it was going to matter. There were just too many agents and not enough of us.

As Minsheng also fired his last trank, he had to duck to avoid being hit himself. Chris readied to throw the last grenade he had, despite how close it would be to us, when Zephyr attacked the two agents that were rushing forward and trying to fire at us.

He used his wings to get more momentum in a run-up and smacked into the first agent from behind, toppling the unfortunate man with a crunch and a yelp that made it clear the agent had a broken bone some-where. Zephyr then barreled into the next agent, springing off the fallen one. The woman went flying back through the doorway.

There was the sound of someone falling and clattering on the stairs before complete silence.

"Fall back," a muffled voice yelled. "Fall back."

I blinked a few times, still feeling groggy enough I wondered if I'd heard it right, but Minsheng got to his feet. Chris handed his gun over a moment later

"I'll stay with Daisy," he said, as he also got to his feet.

I followed, taking deep breaths and looking for some-thing else to eat. I felt wrecked. I spotted a small bag of food with our belongings to grab if we had to run and quickly fished out another energy bar. As soon as it was open, I made my way over to Minsheng and Zephyr, both of them by the door to the warehouse.

The fire had begun to die, the salamanders already out of it and no longer alight. All of them were skittering along the line of windows at the very top of the warehouse and opening them to let the smoke pour out.

Despite that, I coughed as I came out onto the small landing.

Beneath me, agents were grabbing unconscious comrades and dragging them toward the exit, but there were far more down than were left.

"I'm going to give them a hand leaving," I said, using my powers to lift the agents near me. I floated them down to the main floor and then descended myself, Zephyr landing beside me.

The agents glanced nervously my way, but I picked up their fallen comrades again and moved them through the air around the fires and toward the back door.

Some of the maze had caught fire, but the flames there were already mostly out, and I could stand at the far edge and see to the door to drop the agents' bodies in a neat pile.

Minsheng and Zephyr continued to follow me.

We need to get these flames under control, I told Zephyr. *Anything you can do?*

Not directly. If we can find some containers, I can get the salamanders to bring more water down. I nodded.

"Keep an eye on the door," I told Minsheng as I hurried to the kitchens. Pulling out everything that had a handle, I tried to get enough containers for everyone to carry them back and forth.

Chris came to help fill them once he realized what I

was doing, so I ran back with a large bucket to the main source of fire and chucked water on. It hissed and popped angrily, the mats now a charred black lump on the middle of the floor.

As Zephyr and the salamanders brought me fresh water, I aimed it to put out the fire as best I could. Thankfully, with the sprinklers still going, the extra water from us, and the lack of nearby combustible material, it finally died down enough the sprinklers alone were shrinking it.

Putting the container I held down rather than giving it back, I walked toward Minsheng. My Shishou still stood by the broken maze opening, his gun aimed inside.

"They're still collecting their unconscious and wounded," Minsheng whispered. I crouched beside him, keeping to the shadows as I watched some agents reappear and drag off two women who had been downed just after the fire started.

"I want to talk to Knox once this is done. Will you cover me?"

Minsheng looked like he might object to this at first, but eventually, he nodded. I crept forward, explaining to Zephyr and getting him to stay safe.

I'll go keep watch on the roof.

Zephyr's reply brought me more comfort than I'd have liked to admit, and I moved forward a little more. Picking up the last three agents with my powers again, I floated them before me. With the energy bars, I'd regained some strength, but I knew I was going to need something much more substantial once all this was over.

Despite how close to the edge it pushed me, I did my

best to look calm and as if this didn't tax my ability at all. I wanted Knox to think I had plenty more in the tank.

The world outside was brightening, dawn not far off and birdsong sounding from somewhere nearby. It was almost peaceful after the fight of the last couple of hours.

When I was about two-thirds of the way down the alley, Minsheng walking next to my right shoulder with his gun raised, I was noticed. The agents who had returned to get their unconscious colleagues stopped at the end of the alley, then backed up.

I walked to the end as if I had nothing to fear and pretty much deposited the unconscious bodies in the waiting agents' arms. By the time I stepped out of the alley, there was a small ring of agents with their weapons aimed at me. Knox was standing behind a large shield.

"Fire," Knox yelled.

I blasted air out and upward from my position as powerfully as I could. Every dart went off-course, flying overhead. Then I reached toward Knox and used the last of the power I could muster to blow his shield out of his hands from behind. The shield came out of his grasp and clanked into the street, but not before it almost toppled him.

"I wouldn't do that again if I were you," I said. I could only hope the threat had enough demonstration behind it that Knox would take it seriously.

But while defenseless before me and with so few men around him, Knox was sensible for once and motioned for the agents to lower their weapons. He then stepped forward, picking his way through the obstacles, open cars, and barriers they'd hastily erected until he stood just in front of me.

"What do you want? To surrender?" Knox replied.

I laughed and shook my head.

"Take a look around, Knox. Your agents are mostly unconscious and injured, and there's nothing stopping me hurling the rest of them around like rag dolls in a storm right now except my desire to be left alone."

I looked at the agents and noticed them all shifting slightly, looking at their boss as much as me.

"Eight weeks ago, I made a deal with Agent Crawley. Leave me in peace, and I'd cause no trouble. And then you showed up and trashed the place I was staying. I've had enough. Either you go back to wherever you've come from and tell them to leave me alone, or I'll come for them too."

"And if I don't feel like being a messenger boy? I'd rather have you come in for a little chat," Knox asked as if he'd gained a little bravery.

"Try that, and I'm going to see just how far I can blast everything on this street in one go, and then my dragon, the fire salamanders, and I are going to go for a very public walk. We'll see how long the agency building can stand up under the forces at my disposal. Is that clear?"

Knox looked like he might call my bluff for a moment, but eventually, he nodded.

"I'll tell my boss, but I warn you, he doesn't take kindly to being threatened. And we're just one branch of the agency under his control. He's not likely to leave you alone."

"And *I* don't take kindly to being threatened. Neither do I respond well to having yet another home trashed. As I said, if anything even remotely like this happens again, I will come and trash every agency building I can find in the most public manner possible."

"As I said, I'll tell my boss," Knox said as he turned. A moment later, he motioned for the agents to fall back.

I stayed in the alley entrance, watching as the men and women made their way back to vehicles. Very few of them were still moving, more and more injured loaded in passenger seats or in the back of the vans with only a single agent to watch over them all.

Until they were all out of sight, I remained standing in the only entrance to the building.

"Come back inside," Minsheng said a moment later.

I sighed but nodded. I was exhausted.

When I returned to the building, I finally took in its appearance. The maze and the traps were all wrecked, panels broken, and everything else pulled apart. Here and there, Zephyr's breath still lingered, patches of white vapor hanging in pockets near the roof of the maze. The rest had either been burned off by the fire or dissipated by the through-flow of air.

I went around the side of the maze, not wanting to see any more of that destruction, but the stench of the heated mat padding and plastic exterior hit my nose. The fire was out now, and the sprinklers had either been turned off or turned themselves off. In the very middle of the warehouse was a charred, twisted, soggy, black mess.

"That's not coming up off the floor easily," Daisy said as she noticed me.

I smiled, grateful to see she was back on her feet after

being tranquilized. Her assessment was right. I dreaded to think how long it would take to clean the building back up.

There were also spent ammo casings, darts, and several guns on the floor, not to mention marks on the walls and floors where grenades and bullets had chipped the bricks and concrete.

And everything was covered in about an inch of water.

I made my way up to the living area, finding it had only fared better in one respect. There had been no fire in there, but everything was drenched. Chris had managed to retrieve some of our belongings from out of bags and had wrapped them in waterproof jackets. Hopefully, our laptops and phones were among them.

"Have they all gone?" Chris asked as Zephyr came down from the roof.

"Yes," Minsheng replied, but there was no celebration to the declaration. We'd won the battle, but it had cost us almost everything we had.

"That's good because we've got two darts and a grenade left. Maybe a few more rubber bullets, but we weren't sure these last few would fire." Chris righted the table a moment later.

"I'll make us some breakfast," Daisy said. "We should dry out this place as best we can, eat, and then figure out what we're doing next."

I nodded, going to our ready bags to see how much of our clothes and belongings had been soaked through.

CHAPTER TWENTY-FIVE

With full bellies and clothes now drying by warm salamanders, we all sat back and waited for someone to begin speaking. I knew what they'd all want to say. Minsheng had never wanted us to stay anyway, and Daisy and Chris shouldn't have even been part of this fight.

They would want to leave. To go find the Sanctuary. And I didn't blame them.

A huge part of me wanted to leave as well. But I still clung to the hope that we'd be able to stay. That Knox and Crawley would leave us alone after our display of power. After all, we'd managed to best all their combined agents, and they didn't know how much it had cost us.

I was about to open my mouth and speak some of these thoughts when my transceiver came to live, broadcasting sound into the room. I got to my feet and went over to the shelf I'd placed it on. It had been tucked a good way back and had managed to survive the drenching, so I'd set it to play anything in real-time as soon as I'd come up.

It seemed Knox had gotten back.

"You don't look like a victorious man, Knox," Crawley said, adding her voice to the noise of chairs scraping.

"I don't know how many people were inside that warehouse, but by the end of the fight, I only had four of the seventy agents we sent in unharmed and conscious. The rest were knocked out, paralyzed, or injured enough I couldn't send them back in to fight."

"Sixty-six agents? You mean to tell me a girl and her dragon bested sixty-six well-trained people?"

"I'm sure she had help. The agents saw the usual others, some kind of mentor and at least two more with her. And of course, that pesky family of fire salamanders."

"So you just withdrew?"

"Not exactly. She let us walk away. I honestly thought she was going to kill me at one point." Knox sounded deflated, his bravado gone.

There was a silence, and I glanced at the others. They were all listening, no one speaking as we all tried to process what this meant.

"What did you promise her?"

"That I'd speak to Jacobs. She wants him to command that she be left alone."

"He won't agree to that."

"Of course not, but as I said, I thought she was going to kill us. I told her what she needed to hear to let us go. I wouldn't be surprised if Jacobs authorizes lethal force."

"He's asked for an update at nine. We can do it together. I don't think I'm going to be able to explain how you and all our combined agents couldn't sneak into a warehouse and capture a few sleeping mythicals."

"Oh, you'd love that, wouldn't you? You'd love to..." Knox's voice trailed off.

"What? What is it?" Crawley asked, her voice rising in pitch.

"They weren't sleeping," he replied, sounding excited. "They'd boarded up all the doors, prepared traps. They were ready and waiting."

"But how? None of my men knew where they were being sent beforehand."

"Mine either, so don't think you can accuse me of having a mole."

"But if your men didn't know, and my men didn't know, who told them?" Crawley's words were ice-cold, each one formed perfectly and spoken slowly enough the threat behind them was clear.

I bit my lip. It appeared as if they were about to figure out that I had inside information.

"The receptionist? You said she was suspected of giving the girl access to the office the first time," Knox replied.

"No. She's been replaced. But..." Crawley's voice trailed off, and I heard the scrape of a chair, then furniture moving. A moment later, there was a rustling noise as something brushed against the small microphone. They'd found my bug.

I waited for it to be smashed or for it to go dead, but for a moment, there was nothing but silence.

"Well-played, Aella-Faye, well-played," Crawley said a moment later. "I'm going to assume it's you listening to this. I don't know exactly what Agent Knox promised you, but whatever it is, he answers to me, and here's my promise. We're going to be back at that warehouse of yours, and this time there won't be any games or darts you can steal or somehow be unaffected by. There are going to be real guns with real bullets to take out a terrorist because that's what you've become. A threat to the United States of America and its citizens. And I promise you will be met with the full force I have available."

The bug went dead as soon as Crawley had finished speaking. I stepped back, noticing that my hands were shaking.

"We'll have a little while before they come back," Minsheng said, "but I think it's time to go."

I nodded, not daring to argue after the threat of real bullets. Even if I was willing to go up against them, I couldn't risk anyone else's life but my own. Minsheng was right. It was time to go. Perhaps the Sanctuary would have others within it who could help me untangle this mess.

"I can get us a more suitable vehicle and take back the rental van. Make it much harder for us to be tracked," Chris said, already grabbing the van keys and hurrying off.

"I'll gather anything here we'll want to take with us and get the salamanders ready," Daisy added, also hurrying to the exit.

On her way past me, she rubbed my shoulder. I appreciated the gesture and tried to take a deep breath to steady myself. We needed to go, and that meant I needed to decide what had to be done first.

"We should get your books safe," I said to Minsheng, but he didn't move away. Instead, he pulled me into a hug.

"Material things matter to me far less than you and Zephyr. Will you be all right?"

I wasn't sure how to answer at first. Would I be all

right? Yet again, I was being threatened and chased from my home, and all because I'd been led to and then dared to defend a dragon. Looking at Zephyr as he came closer and rested his head on my shoulder, I nodded.

"Zephyr and I are going to be fine, but we need to find somewhere quieter until we both grow stronger."

We'll make them regret this as soon as we are. Zephyr's eyes shone as our gazes met. We'd defend each other, and I didn't doubt that, given enough time, we would both make them regret today.

"Good," Minsheng said. "We'll find the Sanctuary together. And then we'll teach you two everything we can. And let's not forget, as Zephyr matures, he's going to unlock even more memories. Those agents will regret not accepting your offer one day."

With nothing more to be said, we gathered all the items we wanted to bring with us, repacking our bags and putting Minsheng's books into a couple of plastic crates we'd been using for storing ammo and weapons.

Thankfully most of the books were fine. Minsheng had moved them from the usual spot already in case we'd needed to leave, and they'd been kept just about dry enough.

After getting the fire salamanders to help bring all the food stores and everything else down to the back entrance, we all hurried back and forth, making a pile.

I was just dumping a heavy crate of fruit and veggies when Lyra appeared. Her eyes went wide at the destruction behind me.

"Yeah, I know. It's a mess," I said before she could comment.

"What happened?" she asked, coming farther inside and away from the pile so more of the fire salamanders could drop off the groceries they were carrying. The younger ones scampered over to her instead of hurrying off to fetch more.

"The agency worked out where we were and attacked. We survived, but barely."

"I'm so sorry, Aella. I'd have helped if—"

"No," I interrupted her. "It wasn't safe, and it won't be safe. We're going to go find more people like me and see if they can help. I might be gone a while."

"Want me to look after this place while you're gone?" she asked, her eyes shining with the threat of tears. Unable to speak for a moment, I nodded and pulled her into a hug.

"The agents are going to come back. Stay out of their way, but don't let them burn it down if you can help it."

"Understood. I'll get it cleaned up once they realize you're not here and not going to be. Make it look like you've loaned it to me or something."

"Good idea," I replied. "You can use it if you want. For a dojo. Rent it out or something. Use the money how you want."

"You bet. A dojo sounds great."

"You're going to need more mats, though. We kinda...well..." I motioned to the hunk of charred mess in the middle of the room.

Lyra sighed, but soon she chuckled, then we were both laughing. Appearing a moment later, Minsheng gave us a strange look that only served to set us both off again.

By the time we calmed, my sides hurt, and tears were streaming down both our faces. Zephyr and the fire salamanders were also laughing, but I was pretty sure they'd been laughing at our behavior more than with us.

A moment later, Daisy and Minsheng came back with the last of the boxes and all of the bedding we might need to repack into smaller containers. It made me wonder what Chris might be getting us to travel in. We'd acquired a lot of belongings between us, and for the first time, we were going to be leaving somewhere with the option to carry more than a bag each.

I didn't have to wonder for long. Chris pulled up at the end of the alley with an RV. With Lyra, Zephyr, and the salamanders helping, we soon had it loaded with all our belongings.

Chris had outdone himself picking out the vehicle. It wasn't brand new, but there were several sections inside it, and it comfortably slept eight in three areas. The insurance covered him and Daisy under aliases, making my mouth fall open at the fake drivers' licenses he'd been able to obtain in such a short time.

"I've not seen any of this," Lyra said as she shoved the last crate of books and Minsheng maneuvered it underneath the seating and wedged it in so it couldn't slide during transit.

I hugged her once again and then gave her the keys to the warehouse.

"I'll keep it safe for you," she said a moment later. "Make sure you do the same with that dragon of yours. I totally want to see how the world reacts when they find out about him."

I chuckled, not sure they ever would but appreciating the vote of confidence. Part of me wanted to warn her that we might not be back. I had to find the Sanctuary and grow more powerful than the agency and everything they could throw at us, and that wasn't going to be easy. But I couldn't bring myself to say it out loud. It was a doubt, and I couldn't afford to let my doubts grow.

"I'll try to get you a message now and then so you know how I'm doing." I tried to smile as I spoke, but I couldn't bring myself to.

"Only if you can do so safely. I'd rather hear nothing and be able to assume you're still out there kicking ass and taking names than get a message and know the agency was led to you again. Now, go on. Everyone's waiting for you." Lyra moved back and I stepped into the RV.

Minsheng shut the door as Chris started the engine. I found somewhere to sit, grateful Chris and Daisy were up the front and ready to do the driving. I noticed the salamanders were all curled up on the bed above them, and Minsheng was already poring over a book at a small table. I couldn't see Zephyr, so I went to find him.

He was near the back of the vehicle, lying on another double bed that stretched the width of the back. I got up beside him and scooted him over so we could both peek out a side window. Lyra was walking away from the warehouse to her car and didn't see us as we drove away. I sighed.

Think of this as another part of our adventure, Zephyr said in my head.

Where we get to find some mysterious Sanctuary and meet interesting people.

Together.

Always.

EPILOGUE

Sighing, I followed Minsheng down yet another part of the trail, Zephyr at my side. It was early morning and not quite dawn yet, the tall forest around us still gloomy. None of us needed a flashlight, but we couldn't see a long way. Daisy, Chris, and the majority of the salamanders were in the RV, still sleeping.

We, on the other hand, were traipsing through the forest while it was quiet and people were less likely to see Zephyr so we could find an unknown item that might or might not lead us closer to the Sanctuary. I was more than a little grouchy, but I knew it wasn't Minsheng's fault. He was trying to help.

"Remind me again what it is you think we're looking for?" I asked Minsheng as I tripped over another tree root in the dark, only my reflexes stopping me from splatting on my face.

"The Sanctuary members have left markers and items in specific locations for mythicals to find. They're all in obscure places where it's easy to hide, like this forest, and they all guide the finder to the Sanctuary, providing they have the correct DNA to get there." Minsheng didn't stop walking as he explained, and I had trouble keeping up.

I had no idea how he could see so well in this level of light.

Dwarf, Zephyr said in my head, making it clear he'd heard my thoughts. I had barely even been thinking it. Over the last few days, our bond had gotten stronger, and Zephyr was unlocking new memories daily. While the others weren't looking, he'd even practiced talking. Our mental link was far easier, though, and while we were in the crowded RV, we'd used that.

Another twenty minutes passed as Minsheng led us deeper into the forest. The area under the foliage grew lighter, but there was still little color to the surroundings, everything an extremely dark green rather than shades of black and gray. I stubbed my toe again and cursed aloud, making a nearby bird take flight. I jumped again.

Zephyr chuckled, striding ahead until we came to a wider section of the path. A tree had fallen at some point, and someone had used a section of the trunk to carve a bench and place it to one side.

I was about to sit down on it and have a drink when Zephyr walked to the edge of the path and stared into the trees beyond.

"I recognize this place," he said, his voice even deeper than the one in my head. It was the voice of a mature dragon, and it took Minsheng by surprise.

I got up, going to Zephyr's side and looking where he did. Before I could ask him about the memory, he was walking off the path and through the trees. Minsheng pulled out a compass and followed.

Not wanting to be left behind and eager to see what Zephyr thought was out there, I hurried to catch up. Placing a hand on my dragon's back, I walked beside him.

Something about the moment felt somber, almost sacred. I kept quiet so I didn't break Zephyr's concentration. Memories could be slippery. I couldn't imagine how much harder it must be to remember things that weren't his memories.

Eventually, however, Zephyr stopped. He'd found a small clearing in the middle of the forest. A patch of clover grew in the open area. Lifting my eyebrows, I walked into it. My skin tingled as I got closer, but nothing happened once I was in the middle.

"Interesting," Minsheng said. "Something is keeping the trees from growing here and sustaining the clover."

"Something?" I asked. "Or someone?"

It was Minsheng's turn to look puzzled.

"It made my skin feel the same way it does when I control lots of wind at the same time," I explained. "Someone like me did this."

"That would make sense. An elf with an earth affinity would be able to control the forest in a small area."

At Minsheng's words, I slowly rotated on the spot, looking for a shadowy shape that might be doing it. Zephyr chuckled, and even Minsheng smiled.

"What?" I asked.

"They would have put it in place a long time ago," Minsheng explained.

"Oh." Feeling more than a little stupid, I stepped out of

the circle of clover into the darkness by the trees. As soon as I did, Zephyr moved into the clearing and slowly turned on the spot.

What are you looking for? I asked.

This, he replied as he stopped circling and moved toward one of the trees. When he reached the base, he dug at the ground with his front paws, pulling up clover, moss, and other green plants. I came around to the side so I could see what he found as something other than tree roots and plants. A pristine stone container, carved and somehow unsullied, sat in the hole Zephyr had excavated.

I reached for it before Minsheng could, my skin briefly tingling on contact. It gave a *thunk* a moment later, and the lid flicked open. Inside was a strange sphere, a shiny orb made of something dark. I picked it up, the surface cold until it flashed, a deep brown light appearing inside as it warmed up.

The light grew brighter and more focused inside it until it moved to the right of the orb and settled just out of my view. I tried to turn it to get a better look, but no matter which way I turned it, the light stayed in the same place relative to the ground.

It's a compass. Zephyr said in my head. *It's going to lead us to the Sanctuary.*

The story continues with *Dragon Souled,* book 3 in the Dragon of Shadow and Air series.

Claim your copy today!

ACKNOWLEDGMENTS

A massive thank you to everyone at LMBPN, especially Michael for taking a chance on Aella and Zephyr. You're all awesome, and I am eternally grateful.

And to everyone at Variant for helping me bring this story to life, especially Jeff, Jen and Kayla. You've been there right from the beginning when Aella and Zephyr were brand new thoughts, right through to letting the world see into their lives for the first time.

Thank you to Ella for the spit and shine and for helping me with my last minute plot issues.

Also huge thank you to my two main writers buddies, David and Bear for the huge series arc plot discussions. I always come away from our chats excited to get writing and with a much clearer picture of who the villains actually are and what they want.

Thank you to all my discord folks who cheered me on, sprinted with me and generally endured as I worked out who everyone was and what I was doing. You're amazing.

To my husband for giving up so much time during a

global pandemic so I could find a quite place in the house and get these words out. I couldn't have managed to write this during 2020 and all the crap it brought with it without your support.

To my tiny humans for occasionally being asleep.

And to God for the continued understanding and for not making mistakes even if I think you should have made elves real.

ABOUT THE AUTHOR

Jess was born in the quaint village of Woodbridge in the UK, has spent some of her childhood in the States and now resides near the beautiful Roman city of Bath. She lives with her husband, Phil, her two tiny humans (one boy and one girl) and her very dapsy cat, Pleaides.

During her still relatively short life Jess has displayed an innate curiosity for learning new things and has therefore studied many subjects, from maths and the sciences, to history and drama. Jess now works full time as a writer and mummy, incorporating many of the subjects she has an interest in within her plots and characters.

When she's not busy with work and keeping her tiny humans alive she can often be found with friends, playing with miniature characters, dice and pieces of paper covered in funny stats and notes about fictional adventures her figures have been on.

You can find out more about the author and her upcoming projects by joining her on facebook, by watching her live D&D streams, or emailing her via books@jessmountifield.co.uk. Jess loves hearing from a happy fan so please do get in touch!

Jess is also opening up her discord for fans to come chat about what she's up to, and see a few sneak peaks of future work. There's also a chance to become one of her beta readers. If you'd like to check that out you can do so <u>here.</u>

Connect with Jess Mountifield

Mailing list sign up
Facebook group.
Discord group
Actual play D&D stream: Twitch or Youtube
Email address: contact me here.

Books by Jess Mountifield

Urban Fantasy

Dragon of Shadow and Air:

Air-Bound

Shadow Sworn

Fantasy

Tales of Ethanar:

Wandering to Belong (Tale 1)

Innocent Hearts (Tale 2 & 3)

For Such a Time as This (Tale 4)

A Fire's Sacrifice (Tale 5)

Winter Series:

The Hope of Winter (Tale 6.05)

The Fire of Winter (Tale 6.1)

Guild of the Eternal Flame:

Wayfarer's Sanctuary

Protector's Secret

Healer's Oath

Other Fantasy:

The Initiate (under Holly Lujah)

Writing with Dawn Chapman:

Jessica's Challenge (#5 in the Puatera Online series)

Dahlia's Shadow (#6 in the Puatera Online series)

Lila's Revenge (#7 in the Puatera Online series)

Sci-Fi:

Fringe Colonies:

Alliance

Haven

Rebellion

Rebirth

Reclamation

Star Trail:

Hunted

Sherdan series:

Sherdan's Prophecy

Sherdan's Legacy

Sherdan's Country

Sherdan's Road (A short story in the anthology 'The End of the Road')

The Slave Who'd Never Been Kissed (A short in the charity anthology 'Imaginings')

New Beginnings

Santa's Little Space Pirate

In the multi-author Adamanta series:

Episode 1 – Adamanta

Episode 3 – Excelsior

Episode 8 – Phoenix

Episode 13 – New Contacts

Episode 17 – Sacrifice

Other:

Clues, Claws and Christmas

Non-Fic:

How to Write Lots, and Get Sh*t Done: the Art of Not Being a Flake

Find purchase links here

Coming soon:

Urban Fantasy:

Dragon of Shadow and Air:

Shadow-Sworn

Dragon-Souled

Earth-Bound

Fantasy

(Tales of Ethanar):

The Pursuit of Winter (#2 in the Winter series, Tale 6.2)

Books under Amelia Price

Mycroft Holmes Adventures:

The Hundred Year Wait

The Unexpected Coincidence

The Invisible Amateur

The Female Charm

The Reluctant Knight

The Ambitious Orphan

The Unconventional Honeymoon Gift

The Family Reunion

The Immortal Problem

Coming soon:

The Unremarkable Assistant

CPSIA information can be obtained
at www.ICGtesting.com
Printed in the USA
LVHW041141310322
714806LV00006B/1088